The Secrets of Grimoire Manor

by

Christopher J. Ferguson

Grimoire Manor, Book One

The Secrets of Grimoire Manor

COPYRIGHT © 2024 by Christopher J. Ferguson

Contact Information: info@thewildrosepress.com

Cover Art by *Lea Schizas*

The Wild Rose Press, Inc.
PO Box 708
Adams Basin, NY 14410-0708
Visit us at www.thewildrosepress.com

Publishing History
First Edition, 2024
Trade Paperback ISBN 978-1-5092-5599-3
Digital ISBN 978-1-5092-5600-6

Grimoire Manor, Book One
Published in the United States of America

Dedication

To science, our candle in the dark in a demon haunted world (Carl Sagan).
And as ever, to my wife, without whom none of this would be possible.

Chapter 1

Grimoire Manor
October 1
Newport, Rhode Island

Blinking against the glare of the early morning sun, Nevine Turner looked up at the House on Drelock Hill. With its peeling paint and weather-beaten stone arches, it looked more like a prison than a home. Nevine took it all in and tried to think positive. Her caseworker had told her the place turned out well-educated, brilliant young women. Hard to believe. From every turret and tower, every wall, the leering faces of gargoyles and demons stained with mildew and decay stared down at her.

Nevine felt trouble brewing. It wasn't just the architecture, creepy though it looked. Her brain felt electric with the notion that the house was alive. Inside, its halls must have been like arteries coursing with hatred. She swallowed hard. Grimoire Manor would be her home for the next four years until she reached age eighteen.

"Isn't it lovely?" asked her caseworker as she slammed shut the trunk of the car. She handed over a backpack to Nevine, which carried all of her worldly possessions. It wasn't a heavy backpack.

Was this woman retarded or lying? Probably lying

to herself. Nevine was an expert at reading that particular adult facial expression. 'Everything will work out well this time'…'I'm sure an adopted family will finally come through for you this year'…'This foster family truly cares for their children'…it was always the same in the end. "I know," Nevine said. "You think I'll like it once I get used to it."

The caseworker brightened up. "That's the spirit, Nadia."

"Nevine."

"Right. Won't you get the door for me?" The caseworker made to look like she was struggling helplessly with her notepad and pocketbook.

Obscene faces adorned these doors. A great horned bull with the knocker as a ring through its nose stared back at Nevine. Ascending the few stone stairs to the door, Nevine seized the knocker and pounded it against the heavy door several times.

Almost at once, the doors opened outward. For a moment, Nevine wondered if they might have been activated by some kind of electrical lock, like in a hospital. Then both doors slammed open as if pushed and the house belched a great blast of the coldest air. Nevine stumbled backward but managed to catch herself from falling. Air spiraled up around her like a whirlwind, thrashing the ends of her hair against her face. The doors stood open for a moment before they slammed shut. Once again, they opened for a second, gaping like a hungry mouth, and once again they crashed shut with a deafening sound. All was silent.

With trembling hands, Nevine brushed herself off. The caseworker said only, "They must have quite a cross-draft. Now, Nevine, if you would only grip the door more firmly…"

The caseworker must surely be certifiably insane. Still, Nevine did as she was told. She braced herself for the worst. She gripped hold of the handle and pulled with all her might. The door opened without the slightest resistance. As they entered, Nevine expected the door to slam shut once again behind them, but it only quietly clicked into place as if nothing had ever happened.

"Well then, Nevine," said the caseworker, pushing a pair of glasses up the bridge of her nose.

The woman looked about the entry hall of Grimoire Manor, a fake smile plastered to her face. The entrance hall loomed, leading out back to another set of double doors. An immense staircase led up to the second floor, and endless doors beckoned from either side of the main hall leading further into the building. Portraits of sinister and unpleasant elderly people decorated the hallway. The walls and ceiling were elaborately etched. It was both beautiful and intimidating. Had Nevine not somehow been sure that this was the state-run Home for Orphaned Girls, she would have thought she was in the wrong place entirely.

The caseworker clapped her hands together and said, "Here we are. Isn't this exciting that you'll get to live in a mansion?"

Nevine hesitantly stepped forward into the house and glanced around. Her hands still quivered, and her heart remained firmly in her throat. "I think," she said, her voice just a whisper, "that this house hates me."

"What's that, dear?" The tall lady poked at a little gargoyle statue that hung in one corner. "There must be a bell or something around here somewhere."

Nevine ignored her, taking a few more steps into the main hall. She looked up the grand staircase that led up to a landing on the second floor. The carpet leading up the stairs was thinned with age, worn from traffic, and stained in spots.

One of the side doors along the main hall opened and out walked a short old woman, leading a teenaged girl by her shoulders. The white-haired woman wore a sweater and thick glasses, and didn't smile as she cast the new arrivals a distracted glance. The girl appeared to be about fourteen, like Nevine, and had long, straight brown hair and a pretty face. She eyed Nevine warily, though her expression displayed far more interest than that of the old woman.

"Ah," said the caseworker, in hopeful tones, "you must be the director?"

The white-haired woman shook her head and frowned. "You are mistaken. I am Ms. Speer, the head teacher. The Provost is indisposed and has tasked me with receiving our new resident." The old woman turned and frowned at Nevine. "I assume," she said without warmth, "that this is Miss Nevine Turner?"

Nevine opened her mouth, but before she could speak, the caseworker said, "Yes, this is she," as if the girl herself were mute. Nevine and the as-yet-unnamed straight-haired girl exchanged meaningful glances.

The caseworker rummaged through a shoulder bag. "I have her file right here, and of course, you'll need to sign a few things, though most of the arrangements have already been taken care of by the Department of Child Welfare and the…um…Provost." She said this last as if she'd never heard of the woman before.

The white-haired woman reached for the file, handling it with the enthusiasm she'd have shown a used hanky. "Very well then, I'll attend to the remaining matters. Miss Turner, this is Miss Aurora Ziniti, who will be your roommate." The girl with the straight hair gave Nevine a mischievous but friendly smile. "She will show you to your room. You'll wait there until Ms. Emily arrives to show you about the home."

The caseworker clapped her hands and exclaimed in an exaggerated way that made Nevine feel like a child, "Aurora, what a positively eccentric name, just like yours, Nevine! I think you two will become fast friends."

Aurora shot the caseworker a lopsided sneer when she was looking at Nevine, and Nevine suppressed a laugh.

"Perhaps," said Ms. Speer, "you would like a moment to say goodbye to your caseworker, Miss Turner?"

Nevine shrugged and murmured, "Well, I don't really know…"

All at once, she found herself engulfed in the caseworker's arms. "Well then," said the caseworker, hugging her, "this is goodbye. I trust you'll be happy here, and if you need me, you have my card. I'll be back to look in on you periodically and during all major holidays." The caseworker pulled away, giving Nevine a little wave before turning back to Ms. Speer.

Aurora grabbed Nevine's hand and pulled her toward the big staircase, as if escaping from a fire. As Aurora led her up the stairs, Nevine looked back toward the caseworker, curious to see if she was watching them go. The caseworker and Ms. Speer were lost in conversation.

Nevine would never see the caseworker again.

She continued beside Aurora up the stairs and through a long landing to another set of stairs and on to the third level. Nevine blinked at the old decorations that still adorned the place. Over the main landing hung a huge crystal chandelier, now quite dusty and neglected, but still an amazing sight.

Aurora led Nevine through several tight and poorly lit corridors to a second major landing, less well-lit or decorated than the first. Here, the wooden floor was uncarpeted and creaked loudly when they walked on it.

"This was once the servant's quarters," Aurora informed her, the first thing Aurora had said since whisking her away from the adults. Naturally, this was now where the girls were expected to stay, and Aurora opened a door just off the main landing and stepped aside for Nevine.

Nevine found herself in the cramped and dark room that was to be her home for the next four years. Overhead hung a light bulb from a chain with a cloth lampshade meant to try to mask its dreariness. Set across from the door was the room's only truly pleasant feature: a little alcove with a decent-sized window that looked out over the backyard, the Newport cliffs and the ocean beyond.

Nevine rushed over to the window and pulled it open with all her might (and the creaky window did take all her might) enjoying for a moment the cold fresh blast of air that welcomed her efforts.

"Just because it has a nice view," Aurora said from behind her, "doesn't mean you're not in Hell." Nevine turned, a little shocked, and sat on the bed closer to the window, presuming it was hers. "And rest assured, you are in Hell."

There was a small chest of drawers beside each bed and Nevine opened hers and began sorting her few things into the drawers. There wasn't much really: a couple of sets of clothes, a paperback set of the Chronicles of Narnia, and a little stuffed fox. She put the fox on her pillow and a set of mequetaria prayer beads under it. She'd had the fox since she was a little girl, and it was the closest thing she had to a constant companion.

"My advice," Aurora said, watching her, "put the fox where it can't be seen."

Nevine put the fox in one of the drawers. "Would one of the other girls steal it?"

Aurora shrugged. "Of course. And if they didn't, the ghosts would."

Nevine hesitated for a minute, unsure if Aurora was teasing her. "I don't believe in ghosts," she said at last.

Aurora smiled, "Doesn't really matter, does it? So long as they believe in you. And if you don't believe in them now, you will soon." She regarded Nevine with a thoughtful look. "So, are your parents dead or are you a throwaway?" Her words were blunt, but Nevine didn't detect any malice behind them.

"My parents are dead. I never knew them. It happened when I was little. Been in foster care my whole life."

"Me too, although I knew them. We moved here from Florida when I was six and a month later my parents were in a car wreck," she detailed this without emotion, and Nevine guessed that like herself, Aurora had recited her basic background numerous times to the curious. "Well, that's that, then. Boo-hoo." Aurora made a little crying gesture with her fist. "Here's a little hug." She came over and hugged Nevine. "Now we've got that out of the way."

"Did you have a roommate before me?" Nevine asked, testing out the mattress with her hand.

Aurora paused for a moment. "Yes…"

"Hey," Nevine said, "what happened to the girl who lived here before me?"

Aurora got an odd look. She opened her mouth to answer but never got a chance.

A knock at the door sounded at that moment, and it opened before Aurora could respond. A woman, younger and more pleasant looking than Ms. Speer, stood in the doorway. She gave Nevine a little smile and walked into the room, looking about curiously.

"Well, Miss Turner, I see that you have settled in well enough. I'm Ms. Emily and I'll be your teacher for mathematics. This room has a most delightful view of the ocean and you've also benefited from rooming with Aurora Ziniti. She's as solid a roommate as you could have hoped for…" Aurora smiled up at Ms. Emily. "…even if she is given to mischief." Aurora now stuck her tongue out at Ms. Emily when her back was turned. Nevine suppressed a giggle.

"Well, we must get going, Miss Turner. I'm to give you a tour of Grimoire Manor."

"Ms. Emily," Aurora said, her voice taking on the sweet tone of a child who wants something, "would it be okay if I came along too?"

Ms. Emily looked as if she considered it for a

moment before giving them an approving smile. It was the first genuine smile that Nevine had gotten from an adult in a very long time. "I think that would be fine."

Ms. Emily guided them back out to the servant's landing and down the staircase, which was much more rickety and uncertain than the heavy wooden one on the main landing. There were some other girls about now, getting out of classes and preparing for lunch. They regarded Nevine with suspicion.

Ms. Emily whisked them quickly down to a large room in the basement with concrete walls and naked neon bulb lighting in the ceilings. The smell of…something…cooking permeated the vast room. "This," said Ms. Emily, stating the obvious, "is the cafeteria. We have a dedicated staff of cooking personnel and I think that you will find the food served here very nutritious."

Behind Ms. Emily, Aurora made a motion as if to stick her finger down her throat. Nevine smirked.

They went up a small stone staircase into the main hall where Nevine had first entered and then up the central staircase once again. Up to the fourth floor they climbed, where the main staircase ended at a level even with the chandelier's chain. "Here you will find the Provost's office. If you remain well-behaved, you shan't have to meet with her too often. Miss Ziniti," — and here Ms. Emily gave the other girl a little smirk— "has made her acquaintance once or twice." Aurora frowned.

"Please be sure not to rush up to the attic without a teacher accompanying you. The lighting is not good up there, and sometimes vermin go there to roost." She walked over to a set of double doors that were padlocked shut. "Unfortunately, the west wing of the building is currently off limits to exploration as well."

"Oh," said Nevine, "is that because that's where the ghosts live?"

Aurora's eyes went wide, and she gave Nevine a shocked but amused look.

Ms. Emily turned around slowly and looked Nevine over very carefully before answering. "The west wing is closed because there has not been enough money to properly renovate it. The floors are very weak and likely to collapse under the weight of anyone walking on them. The ghosts," Ms. Emily said with a raised eyebrow, "feel free to walk about anywhere within the house."

Nevine laughed a little, as Ms. Emily seemed to be having a little fun with them. She wasn't quite sure if there was an undercurrent of seriousness beneath the jest. Aurora, for her part, was not laughing.

Ms. Emily turned away, leading them back down the main staircase. "Should you get it in your head that it might be an adventure to explore the west wing, which many children seem to do simply because they've been forbidden to do so, be assured you won't have been the first. The penalties for doing so are, as you might suspect, quite stern."

Nevine and Aurora exchanged raised eyebrows. Nevine suspected that Aurora had been one of those making past attempts.

"As you will have noticed," Ms. Emily said as they descended the stairs, "there are no televisions, no video games, no radios, no cell phones…"

"…no good food, no hot baths, no fun, but plenty of rats," Aurora whispered on the side.

"…Grimoire Manor is dedicated to your education and we hope that it will serve its purpose in preparing you to become responsible adults in an outside world that is quite filled with all manner of temptations and hostilities." They were on the first floor again now, in the main hall. "Aurora, I think you can resume your duties as hostess? It's time for lunch, and I have other matters to see to."

"Yes, Ms. Emily," Aurora said, dutifully.

"Very well then, Miss Turner, I'll wish you good luck and I'll see you in math class." She gave Nevine a little wink and a smile before turning. She walked away down the main hall and into one of the little side doors.

"Well," said Nevine with a shrug, "she didn't seem too bad."

"Yeah," Aurora said with a meaningful frown. "She's the nice one."

Nevine walked back to the main staircase and stood looking up at the chandelier. "Did people really live here once?"

"People live here now," Aurora smiled.

A sound like a boulder smashing into the roof echoed throughout the house, a deep angry sound that seemed to come from the very walls. Crash after crash ensued, one sound after another vibrating through the walls, six or seven of these thunderous reverberations coming perhaps a second apart. Terrified, Nevine rushed to Aurora's side, gripping the other girl tightly. She looked all about with wide eyes, but couldn't tell where the noise was coming from. As they rang out she felt that this house, whatever torments it had inflicted on the other girls who lived here, had decided to hate her most of all. At last, the noises stopped, and she realized she had been holding her breath.

"What," Nevine asked, still looking about for some explanation, "was that?"

"Oh, well," said Aurora, her voice full of bravado, "the house sometimes makes sounds like that. It's an old house. The teachers say that air gets into the pipes and bangs about. Come on, we should get to lunch."

The other girl's bravery made Nevine feel better. She was too frightened to notice that Aurora had been gripping her arms as tightly as Nevine had been gripping hers.

Chapter 2

The Power of Words

Lunch sucked, there was no other way to put it. Nevine didn't want to think about what kinds of toxic nastiness she had just forced into her heaving and panicking stomach. The only thing that could be said positively about the lunch experience was that Aurora introduced Nevine to a couple of the other girls. Clarisse was tall, dark-skinned, and self-assured, whereas Polly was small and bookish. Nevine didn't feel close to either of them as quickly as she had with Aurora. Clarisse talked about sports a lot and Polly mostly just complained. They seemed nice enough, though, and welcomed her.

After lunch, the girls were let outside for an afternoon recess. Aurora went to use the bathroom, leaving Nevine with Polly and Clarisse. The air was cold, but it felt good against Nevine's skin. A powerful breeze was blowing in off the ocean and she could smell the salt from the sea.

Clarisse was still griping to Polly about the lack of a good softball team. Since this conversation didn't really appeal to Nevine, she excused herself to get a better look at the cliffs through the chain-link fence. She wandered between two of the big shrubs that hid the fence. These shrubs were obviously meant to hide the ugly fence. Rings of barbed wire at the top complicated escape over the fence if anyone were so inclined.

Nevine pushed her face up to the fence and hooked her fingers through the links. From here she couldn't see very well over the cliff, but down below she could spy some of the jagged rocks jutting out of the sea. Cold seawater foamed and crashed against the rocks. She gave a little sigh at the view.

"Well, what is this?" came a voice from behind her. Startled, Nevine spun around and found herself face to face with two girls of her age. One of them was very tall and athletic, like Clarisse, the second shorter, a blonde-haired girl with blue eyes and porcelain skin. The second girl was very beautiful, like a girl on a TV show or movie. It was this porcelain-skinned girl who spoke. She smiled at Nevine, but there was something sinister and unwelcoming in her expression. "We have someone new here at Camp Grimoire."

The girls laughed a bit, leaving Nevine to wonder if they were laughing at her, or at some kind of inside joke. She smiled and laughed nervously, not wanting to be left out.

"What's your name?" the blonde girl asked.

"Nevine Turner."

"I'm Fiona. This," —she thumbed over her shoulder at the big girl— "is Jo-Beth and YOU are on OUR territory." A few other girls gathered behind Fiona and Jo-Beth, lesser girls who hovered around them like vultures. Nevine looked around to see what kind of lousy position she had put herself in.

Only one teacher was supervising the recess, and she was attending to another girl, who appeared to have a sprained ankle. The way that girl kept peering over at them led Nevine to suspect it was a planned distraction. None of the older girls, who Nevine thought might help, were nearby, either. Aurora was still nowhere to be seen. She was on her own.

"I, uh…" Nevine mumbled, not quite sure what to say. She moved away from the fence, giving herself a bit more room. This was hardly the first time she had found herself in a turf war with another girl and she knew how to prepare herself. The trouble was that Jo-Beth, sidekick of Fiona's, was much bigger than she. If this got ugly, it wasn't going to be a fair fight.

"Don't speak much?" Fiona asked, cruelly seizing upon Nevine's unsure pause. "What kind of girl are you anyway?" Jo-Beth lazily chuckled at Fiona's taunts.

"What do you mean?" Nevine's heart pounded.

Fiona stepped up to her with an almost disgusted look on her face, "Just like I asked: what kind of girl are you? I mean, look at you—curly black hair, your skin looks like it hasn't been washed in a month."

Nevine was used to meanness in others, but this was an unusually cruel assault on her appearance, even for what she had come to expect. "This is my normal skin color! My mother was Egyptian, a Copt!" she protested with shock and anger, reciting what caseworkers had told her through the years. In truth, she didn't really know what a Copt was but she was hardly going to admit that now.

Fiona scoffed at this, looking back at Jo-Beth for the other girl's reaction. "Do you hear that? She says her mom was a cop," Fiona sneered. "Say whatever you want, but to me, you look just like a…" And then Fiona called Nevine a name that no one should ever be called.

Without thinking, without realizing it, she watched as her fist arced away from her shoulder and connected harshly with a very surprised Fiona's mouth. She regretted it a little in the second afterward, regretted letting her anger get the best of her. It was satisfying to see Fiona's expression, though.

"She hit me!" Fiona cried out in shock. Then the shocked look on Fiona's face turned to pure hatred. She leapt onto Nevine, and they were pulling and yanking at each other's hair. Fiona lost her balance but managed to pull Nevine down with her. She rolled around on the ground with the blond girl, a handful of hair in one hand while she punched with the other. Fiona punched and scratched in turn, aiming for Nevine's face. Jo-Beth stood just behind the blond girl, kicking whenever she got an opening. Nevine felt the big girl's shoe crash into her hip, and then slam into the side of her face. There was no way, she realized, that she could fight them both…she was doomed.

All at once, a loud scream rent the air, like a war cry. Something landed on Jo-Beth's back, pulling her chin back by the neck. Nevine caught a glimpse of Aurora's hair in what became a second writhing, confused jumble of girls. Her heart lifted just a bit before Fiona's fist crumpled any enthusiasm she had.

Even with Aurora's help, Nevine had her hands full. Fiona's fists pummeled her, and though she struck back with all her might, she couldn't seem to get the upper hand. A crowd of girls began to gather, watching them with amusement. Some of Fiona's lesser friends were looking antsy, as if they might have joined in, but by now Clarisse and Polly had gotten closer too and they were held at bay.

Nevine was quickly becoming tired from all the wrestling around. Fiona seemed to be getting tired as well, but the rage in the other girl's eyes made it clear that the fight wasn't going to end soon on its own. The gathered circle of girls had drawn the attention of the teacher, however; as such, a circle could only mean one thing. Nevine was dimly aware of the circle scattering and suddenly there were hands on her and Fiona, pulling them off the ground and pushing them apart. Aurora and Jo-Beth had already been separated, and an older girl stood between them. Both of the other girls looked ready to continue the fight, and Fiona still wore a hateful sneer as she wiped away some blood that trickled from her lip.

"You've just asked for a lot of trouble, Cop-Girl!" she growled.

"All right, that's enough from the lot of you," the old teacher screeched. "What has gotten into you girls? You're rolling around in the dirt like a bunch of savage…boys!" The woman glared at the four girls, none of whom responded, busy catching their breath and trading ugly looks.

The teacher plucked Jo-Beth and Fiona by their collars and began escorting them back inside. She instructed the older girl, a senior, "You take those other two to Ms. Emily. She'll know what to do with them."

The senior, whose name Nevine later learned was Victoria Turnbell, didn't look as if she enjoyed the task. Still, she cast a disapproving look at Nevine and Aurora. "You should just have a look at yourselves," she said with a shake of her head. "All right, let's go then and find Ms. Emily."

Nevine had liked Ms. Emily well enough and

looked over at Aurora hopefully, but Aurora was looking both angry and glum. Nevine could only sigh as they were led back into Grimoire Manor to meet their fate.

****

Twenty minutes later, Nevine and Aurora were sitting quietly in an otherwise empty classroom. They had been brought to Ms. Emily, who had listened to Victoria Turnbell's account of what had occurred. Ms. Emily had listened to the story, the icy look in her eyes a warning to the girls to keep quiet.

At last, Victoria was dismissed, and Ms. Emily had turned on the two girls. Her eyes bored into Nevine. "Exactly how long have you been here, Miss Turner?"

"Emm…" said Nevine, squirming in her seat. "…I think maybe an hour?"

"I'll be generous and give you an hour and a half, and already you've found yourself a cupboard full of trouble." She looked over at Aurora. "I rather expect this kind of behavior from Aurora, who can be, as we say, a hothead, but I had hoped that you might have proved a calming influence for her. I see that my hopes were misplaced." Ms. Emily seemed to chew on her own tongue for a moment. "Wait here for a minute," she said at last.

Ms. Emily had left the room, leaving them in the quiet of their own thoughts.

Nevine shifted restlessly, not sure if they would be in more trouble if they dared to speak. She could only take it for so long, though, and said at last, "Thank you for helping me."

Aurora grinned, her face covered with dirt and grass. "I couldn't have very well left you on your own with those brutes, now could I? I should have told you that Fiona and Jo-Beth are jerks. Nice jab, by the way."

Nevine grinned back, looking at her hand where the knuckles were now swollen. "How much trouble do you think we'll be in?" she asked.

"A lot," Aurora said with a nod, "but it was worth it."

Ms. Emily whooshed back into the room carrying two heavy books. She let each one o crash down on the desks in front of Nevine and Aurora.

"What are these?" Nevine asked, looking at the big dusty tome.

"*War and Peace*, by Tolstoy." As she said this, she placed a lined notebook of the sort used for essay questions and a pen in front of each girl. "You are to copy the first thirty pages, in entirety, by hand, before you are to leave this room." Nevine heard Aurora's head hit the desk. "If you begin now, you may have a chance to finish in time for dinner, which ends at six-thirty."

"Ms. Emily," Nevine said, raising her hand habitually as she spoke, "you can't…eh…legally…refuse to feed us…can you?"

Ms. Emily put her hands on her hips and fixed her with a furious glare. "I think you will find that many of the privileges to which you've become accustomed no longer apply here at Grimoire Manor!" She paused, her facial expression softening a bit. "If you miss dinner, we'll find something for you, although I assure you it will be cold and tasteless. What on Earth possessed you to hit Fiona Applegate?" Nevine repeated what Fiona had said to her, and even Aurora, who had not yet heard the whole story, looked shocked.

"I see," Ms. Emily said. "Well, I am well aware of Miss Applegate's nature and you can be assured that she and her cohort are receiving a similar punishment, but still that gives you no right to hit her. Now, I think you have some copying to attend to." Ms. Emily moved to leave the room, but she paused before closing the door. "I hope you know that if you ever have trouble with any of the other girls, you can always come to me."

Nevine was touched by her words. "Ms. Emily, if I tattled all my problems to you, they'd just bully me harder. You know that, don't you?" Off to the side, Aurora was nodding approvingly.

Ms. Emily's eyes were downcast. "Yes, I know that. But what else am I supposed to tell you?" Not looking at the two girls, she closed the door.

****

The two weary girls didn't return to their room until 9 p.m., their wrists cramped and swollen, their immediate needs wrestling between eating and sleep. Grimoire Manor was quieted down by that time, although lights still shone under the doors of some of the girls' rooms. Nevine and Aurora collapsed in their beds, each of them sore in so many places.

"So," Aurora asked, her mouth half muffled by her pillow, "how did you like your first day at Grimoire Manor?"

Nevine smiled and then started laughing, rolling over on her back so she could get enough air to laugh as hard as her body wanted to. Aurora started laughing as well, and their mirth was infectious and unstoppable. When they finally settled down, Nevine reached into her drawer and found the stuffed fox there. She had half expected it to be missing already, the way her day had gone. She clutched the little stuffed animal to her chest, enjoying the closeness with something so soft. It was a childish gesture, but this was the only thing that was like a family to her.

Victoria Turnbell knocked on their door a few minutes later and brought them in a tray with two bowls of cold porridge and a pitcher of orange juice. "Here's a little sustenance for Thelma and Louise," she said with a smirk.

"Huh?" Nevine and Aurora said simultaneously.

"Never mind," Victoria said with an exasperated look. She set the tray down on the night table between the cots. Victoria took the little chair by Aurora's desk, apparently intent on watching them as they ate.

Nevine was almost too tired to eat, but she forced her wobbly arms to scoop the gruel into her mouth. As Ms. Emily had promised, the porridge was further punishment for their behavior.

"You wanna bite?" Aurora asked, with a slightly challenging tone, obviously wanting to know why Victoria was hovering around.

Victoria shook her head. "You know, as much as you two dislike Fiona and Jo-Beth, in all probability, you're going to have to live with them for the next four years."

Aurora's head collapsed on her pillow as if the last embers of energy had been stolen from her. "I must have been a bank robber in a past life."

Nevine smiled at Aurora, but her eyes narrowed at Victoria. "I'm not the one who out of the blue called someone a...a...."

Victoria nodded. "I know perfectly well what

Fiona Applegate's type is like, and if she weren't here, there'd be another girl just like her to take her place. If it makes you feel any better, last I heard Fiona and Jo-Beth were still writing. Some people are going to go through life fighting. Do you want to be like that?"

Aurora put her hands on her hips. "I'd rather that than be a coward all my life."

Victoria shook her head again. "Well listen. Ms. Ellis seems to think that you two might be salvageable. Since I've got good grades and a good disciplinary record…and since no good deed goes unpunished, she's asked me to mentor you two." She paused, waiting for a response.

Nevine and Aurora blinked, staring at her.

Victoria let her face fall into her palm for a moment before saying, "Why don't we plan on spending Sunday evenings together? We can talk, I can help you with homework, and I'll tell you what I've learned so far about how the world works."

Nevine and Aurora looked at each other and then nodded to Victoria. Nevine figured they didn't really have any more pressing plans, after all.

"All right then," Victoria said, standing and moving toward the door. "You had better get cleaned up and ready for bed." Nevine heard a note of fear creep into her voice. "it will be ten o'clock soon." She closed the door behind her.

"What happens at ten o'clock?" Nevine asked once Victoria had left.

Aurora's eyes narrowed. "They shut off all the hall lights…and then the ghosts come out."

"No way!" Nevine giggled, although Aurora didn't join her. She gulped nervously and rushed to the washroom before all the lights went out.

****

Though she was exhausted, sleep eluded Nevine that night. This was probably to be expected, given all that had happened in the past twelve hours. She was settling into a new place and while she had already found a new friend, she appeared also to have earned herself a formidable enemy as well. Her stomach grumbled as the porridge didn't really fill her up, her wrist was cramped from writing, and her cheek and ribs hurt from where Jo-Beth had kicked her.

She tried listening to the waves down below the cliff, which she could hear very well through the window. Their crashing was more violent than soothing. Her eyes wandered around her new room. With the lights out, there seemed to be looming shadows everywhere.

From outside the hall, she could hear footsteps in the hall, slowly moving across the landing. One by one, the sounds brought creaking protests from the old and dry wood. Nevine held her breath for a moment, listening to the footfalls. One of the teachers probably, making rounds of the girls' rooms. That sort of thing was quite normal in places like this, and Nevine was accustomed to it. She listened to the steps for a moment, noting as they moved past the door.

For some reason, she sat up then, feeling oddly electrified. She looked over at Aurora and saw that the other girl had the blankets covering her head. "Aurora," she called out in a whisper, "are you awake?"

"Shhh!" Aurora hissed back.

"What's wrong?"

"It's the Hallway Ghost, now be quiet or it will

hear us!" Aurora sounded quite serious, but Nevine was having trouble believing her.

"There's no such thing as ghosts!" she insisted.

"Do you want to go out there and see for yourself?" Aurora challenged, pulling the blanket down far enough that Nevine could see her frown.

Nevine felt a wave of frustration hit her. "That's exactly what I'm going to do!" she decided to Aurora's obvious horror, "and I'll show you that it's just a teacher or one of the girls going to the bathroom." She threw the blankets aside and leapt from the bed. Outside, she could still hear the slow footsteps moving down the landing, away from their room.

Aurora pulled the blankets away from her face completely now. "No, Nevine, don't be stupid!"

But Nevine was quite determined by now, marching over to the little door, intent on proving to Aurora...or indeed herself, that there was no ghost there. "Aurora, it's just a story they tell you to keep you in bed, I'm sure. Look, I'm going to prove it to you. There's no one out here but..." She pulled open the door, stepping out into the hall mid-sentence.

As soon as she opened the door, the air felt different, like it was deader or deprived of oxygen or something. Nevine's breath felt as if it was pulled out of her lungs and she made a sound like a long, tortured sigh. She could only suck her breath back in with effort. She could feel the hairs on her arms and the back of her neck begin to stand up.

Down the hall on the wooding landing where she had just heard the footsteps and had expected to see a teacher or one of the other girls...was nothing, nothing at all. The landing looked just as it had before, only much darker, of course. The air, though, it just felt wrong, like the air in a tomb that had been robbed. The sounds of the footsteps had stopped.

"Nevine..." Aurora called out softly, "...are you okay..."

Nevine tried to respond but found she couldn't; could only make a little breathing sound. She was rooted to the spot, paralyzed and unable to move, her eyes staring at the blank spot in space where a person was supposed to be.

Then, at once, one of the floorboards creaked. Nevine saw the board move downward a bit as if under some weight—invisible weight. It was a long, soft sound, as though a person had tentatively stepped forward, testing the beam in fear that it might break. Nevine stared at that spot, her eyes wide. Her heart was pounding so hard in her chest that it seemed about to rip free. She struggled again to suck in a breath. Nothing moved for a second, not Nevine, not that board on the floor...and then it relaxed, moving upward with another creak as if someone were stepping off it. At the same time, another floorboard creaked. ...and this one was closer to their room. It was as if...okay, Nevine thought, the ghost...had turned around and was moving back toward her.

Finally, Nevine broke free of her paralysis and ran back into the bedroom, slamming the door shut. She ran over to her bed and leapt onto it, fishing under her pillow for the prayer beads, clutching them close to her chest. She stared at the door for a moment before realizing the door had no lock.

"What did you see?" Aurora hissed.

Nevine ignored her and jumped back off the bed,

and grabbed one of the little chairs near the desks. She braced it up under the doorknob the way she had seen people do on television. Then she ran back to the bed and pulled the covers up to her chin.

Aurora didn't pester her anymore for information, and instead, both girls held their breath as the sound of footsteps moved back down the landing toward their doorway. The sounds stopped right outside their door. A moment later, the doorknob jiggled back and forth, and something attempted to push the door open, but it would not budge against the chair.

Both girls screamed at the top of their lungs...and they kept screaming and screaming, terrified out of their wits. The door stopped moving inward against the chair, and the girls stopped screaming, taking deep breaths to calm their nerves. Then suddenly the door slammed against the chair with more force and almost moved it out of the way. Nevine and Aurora erupted in fresh screams.

"Nevine, Aurora!" called a voice from beyond the door, and now the two girls could see Victoria's face through the crack she had opened. "What's going on?"

Nevine and Aurora both jumped off their beds and ran to the door, pulling the chair out of the way. As Victoria stepped inside with a puzzled look, they leapt into her arms, sobbing with relief.

****

It was well past midnight before Victoria managed to calm the two girls down. Nevine appreciated that Victoria listened to their story patiently and without trying to convince them that it had only been their imagination. After the story was done, Victoria sighed, went back to her room and returned with a pillow and blanket. Closing the door behind her, Victoria settled down on the floor between the two cots. "Now try to get some sleep, girls. If there are any ghosts out there, they're going to have to come through me first."

Nevine thanked her and settled down into her bed, although her heart was still racing. She couldn't believe that she had actually seen…well, not seen…a ghost. How was she ever going to get to sleep tonight after that?! She didn't think it was going to be possible. At least the ghostly footsteps were gone, and Victoria was here to protect her. Sure, Victoria was just another girl like them, but she was older and wiser and, hopefully, braver. The ghost had gone away when she had arrived.

Nevine went back to looking around the room, wishing she could sleep. After a timid 'good night', Aurora rolled over and buried her head in the blankets. Victoria seemed to go to sleep quickly, leaving Nevine feeling alone once more. The sound of Victoria's breathing was comforting, though, and she decided to count the breaths one after another. She was still doing this when, finally, in the middle of the night, she fell asleep.

Chapter 3

The City of a Hundred Spires

Nevine woke up feeling very cold and was shivering uncontrollably. Despite the darkness, she still felt sleepy and attempted to pull the blankets tighter against her neck, only to discover she wasn't covered at all. She opened her eyes and looked around. She glanced up and saw stars twinkling from between what looked like two rather tall buildings. Alarmed, she sat up and gazed all around.

She noticed several things at once. First, she was lying on the ground in what appeared to be some kind of alleyway. Second, there were perhaps two inches of snow covering the ground. Third, she was no longer wearing her pajamas but instead dressed in some kind of thick, frilly dress and overcoat, stockings, and boots. These were not her clothes at all, but something you might see in an old painting...even the teachers weren't old enough to go around wearing this kind of clothes.

She stood up and brushed dirt and snow off herself. She immediately suspected that Fiona Applegate had played some kind of trick on her, although she couldn't explain how Fiona had made it snow in October. Disoriented at not recognizing her surroundings, although this alley didn't look like anything she had noticed at Grimoire Manor, she couldn't hear the waves crashing against the beach anymore.

Pulling her overcoat more tightly around her, she ventured out of the narrow lane into the larger street beyond. Here she could see the buildings more clearly, and most of them appeared to be perhaps five or six stories tall, packed close together, and were of a design she had never seen before. She was in some kind of city, but the buildings looked…old. Many had portions along the face that jutted out from the main building, and almost all featured vaunted statues or gargoyles, and a variety of black or gold spires at the top, as if they were wearing hats. The street was narrow, barely wide enough to fit a single car, let alone two lanes of traffic, and made of cobblestone. Every so often, some streetlamps flickered with open flames rather than humming steadily with electric bulbs.

She stepped out further into the empty street to get her bearings. Not too far away, she could see the enormous stone walls of a fortress towering over this part of the city. Beyond the walls, she didn't see a castle, but she could make out the spires of some kind of cathedral. At the moment she could see no one else on the streets, and aside from the streetlamps, the city was dark.

What's going on? She considered the possibility she might be dreaming, yet she tended to believe her dreams were real while she was having them. This seemed too real, even for that. She had seen someone pinch themselves on a cartoon once to escape a dream and tried this, but it didn't make the city go away.

She walked around in a little circle looking for something that would make sense, or would explain what was going on. If this wasn't a dream, she didn't know what to do in a strange city. Where would she sleep? How would she get food?

"Hello!" she finally called out, tentatively at first. She felt bad waking people up in the nearby buildings, but as her fear built, she called out again, "Heeellooooo! Can somebody help me?"

At first, she got no response, but then, far down the street, she heard something moving. It might have been footsteps, but it made a somewhat awkward sound, kind of a *step...shhhlooop,.....step...shhhlooop*...over and over again, moving slowly and deliberately in her direction. Nevine turned to look for it, but it was hard to see much in the darkened city.

At last, she saw something pass under one of the streetlamps. It looked like a man wearing a cape and some kind of top hat, but only saw his shadow—the light never illuminated his face. He looked to be partially dragging his left leg, which made the *shhhlooop* sound. Nevine was quite certain that he lumbered in her direction, slowly and deliberately. Something about him felt sinister, maybe because he didn't call back or wave, or maybe because she only saw his shadow.

"Hello?" she called out again, although her voice was more uncertain now. A really bad feeling came over her, making the hairs on her neck and arms stand up, just like when she had encountered the ghost on the landing. She took a few steps backward, away from the man.

When he saw her retreat, he immediately broke into a run, silently and swiftly moving toward her. At first, it surprised her that he could move so fast with that bad leg of his. There was no doubt about his intentions; he rushed for her menacingly, with obvious intent to do her harm.

Nevine screamed and broke into a run, moving as fast as she could down the unfamiliar street away from him. She wasn't used to the boots she wore and kept stumbling as the toes got caught in the cobblestones. Fear sent adrenaline coursing through her veins and she ran faster than she ever had in her life.

She couldn't believe this was happening...couldn't really understand *what* was happening. Her encounter with the ghost had been weird and scary enough...and now this! She didn't know what to think about waking up in some strange-looking and unfamiliar city, being chased by this horrible man. What had she ever done to deserve all of this?

She ran as fast as she could along the street, unsure where she was going. She remembered hearing somewhere that if she was being chased, she shouldn't look behind her because she would slow down or maybe trip. With that thought in her mind, she tried hard not to look behind but to keep on running. She was sure he was gaining on her somehow. She could almost feel his horrible hands about to close around her neck and strangle the life out of her. It became harder to see what was in front of her as tears tumbled, clouding her vision. The freezing air whipped, causing her eyes to feel cold and in need of blinking.

At last, she could take it no more and looked behind her. The frightening man was only a few seconds away. She still could not make out his features, cloaked in darkness as he was, and making no sounds aside from those of his foot and bad leg against the pavement. His hands reached out, trying to grasp the edges of her cloak.

As she stared wide-eyed, she suddenly collided against something soft but unmoving, and she tumbled hard on her butt. Feeling trapped and doomed, she looked up to see that she had collided with a woman with long black hair in a woolen cloak. It was too dark to see the woman's face well, but she was staring down at Nevine and yelling at her. Nevine couldn't understand what the woman was saying. It sounded like a foreign language.

"I don't understand!" Nevine cried, looking behind her at the shadow man.

"You speak English?" the woman said with an odd accent. "Get behind me at once!"

Although more confused, she did as told. The woman didn't seem to want to hurt her, and that was enough for the moment. She clutched fearfully at the woolen cloak and looked back at the shadow man still pursuing her, his arms outstretched toward both her and the strange woman.

The woman reached into her cloak and withdrew a tube that was about a foot long. Acting quickly, she pulled some kind of cap off of the tube and held it high above her head. Instantly, the little section of the city they were in was bathed in a brilliant red light, as if it were almost the middle of the day. The little tube in her hand was sizzling and crackling and giving off the brilliant red light.

The shadow man stopped running suddenly and held his hands up as if to protect his face from the light. Nevine could somewhat see his hands now. The skin on them looked very rough, brown perhaps, and areas appeared to be peeling away from the bones underneath. The fingers ended in thick-looking talons like a carnivorous bird. These, had they gotten onto Nevine, could have ripped her to shreds.

"Stay behind me!" the woman demanded, although Nevine had no intentions of doing otherwise. The woman reached into her cloak with her free hand and pulled out a strange-looking little pistol. Unlike the pistols Nevine had seen in the movies, this one looked like it had four different barrels arranged in a little cluster, like pencils held together with a rubber band. The woman pointed it at the shadow man and yelled at him in that strange language.

The shadow man didn't reply. Even now, cringing away from the tube's red light, he made not a sound. It seemed clear that, if not for the light, he would resume his charge.

The woman fired the little pistol, and a loud crack reverberated through the city. Nevine heard the little bullet sing through the air and whack into the shadow man. He tumbled backward a few steps, still not making a sound. The woman appeared ready to fire again and finally, the shadow man turned and ran with his odd but fast limping run back up the street from where he had come.

The woman put the pistol back in her cloak, and with the fiery cylinder still raised over her head, she grabbed Nevine's hand. Her fingers were strong, yet also brought warmth to Nevine's cold hand. "Come with me," the woman insisted, urgency in her voice. She pulled Nevine after her, running along the streets away from the shadow man. After a few minutes, the tube suddenly stopped glowing, and the woman threw it in the street. For a few minutes more, they kept running without a word between them before the woman pulled her into another alley and stopped to inspect her.

"You are all right?" the woman asked, looking Nevine over for any wounds.

"I think so," Nevine said, shivering with cold now that her adrenaline was wearing off. "Where am I? Who was that man? Who are you?"

"You must be lost," said the woman, seeming satisfied that Nevine was unharmed. "We are near Vysehrad Castle." She gestured up at the stone walls where Nevine had seen the cathedral spires. "That man, if he can be called such a thing, is the Ghoul of Vysehrad, and you were fortunate that I was tracking him, or he would have killed you for certain. As for myself, I am Xanthae Halruaa, physicist and ghost-hunter," she said proudly.

Now that Nevine had a better chance to look at her benefactor, she could see that Xanthae was perhaps in her thirties with a pretty face that seemed to consist mainly of big, dark eyes and hair so untamed as to seem almost uncombable.

The woman was proudly rattling off her accomplishments. "I am the first woman to earn a Ph.D. in physics from Charles University, and I hold an appointment as Imperial Astronomer for Emperor Franz Joseph…" She coughed and her eyes got a little wide as she realized she was going on. "But who are you? You are lost? I can take you to your family if can you tell me how to find them." Thankfully, her English was very good, if rather accented.

"I'm Nevine Turner and I don't know where I am," she said. "I don't know how I got here, and my parents have been dead for a very long time. I'm supposed to be at Grimoire Manor in Newport and I really should be getting back there. I'm going to be in more trouble than I already am if they find me missing!"

"Newport," the strange woman repeated. "That sounds like a British city...you are English?"

"No, I'm American," she exclaimed. She could feel fresh hot tears welling up in her eyes and turned away, not wanting to look like a child in front of this stranger.

"It will be all right," assured the woman, patting her shoulder. "Calm down. American you say...do you mean Newport, Rhode Island? I have heard of that." She gently guided Nevine by the shoulder and continued walking down the street. Nevine guessed the woman didn't want to remain in that spot too long in case the shadow man...the Ghoul...came back. She didn't protest as she really didn't know where else to go, and was grateful to have the woman helping her.

"Yes!" Nevine cried. "That's where I need to be!"

"Well," said the woman, looking confused and chuckling a bit, "you are nowhere near there and it will be very difficult to get you back. Do know you where you are now?"

"You said I was near some kind of Visual Castle."

"Vysehrad Castle. We are in the City of Prague," the woman explained.

"Is that in Connecticut?" Nevine asked hopefully.

"No." Xanthae laughed, although Nevine could hear concern in her voice. "Prague is in Bohemia." She waited for recognition from Nevine, and seeing none, explained further, "Most beautiful city in the Austro-Hungarian Empire!"

"Austria?" Nevine cried, "but...that's like, in Africa!"

"Europe, dear," Xanthae corrected her, patting her head. "What do they teach you in America today?" Stopping their forward movement, she knelt next to Nevine again, stroking her hair. Nevine could tell that Xanthae was checking for a head injury. Finding none, she seemed to give up and looked Nevine in the eyes. "Say you have no parents? And say you have no place in Prague that you should be other than this Grimoire Manor in Newport, Rhode Island, America?"

Nevine got a little confused by the way Xanthae spoke, but shook her head. A single hot tear rolled down one of her cold cheeks.

"Well then," Xanthae said, standing back up, "come with me tonight and be my guest. Tomorrow, we figure out what to do with you. I live there," —she pointed up at the Vysehrad Castle walls— "in the Imperial Observatory on the old castle grounds. I think you will like it there."

"Thank you," Nevine said and hugged Xanthae's waist.

"You are feeling hungry?" the woman asked as they resumed walking.

"Yes, yes! I am very hungry." Nevine looked up at her after a moment. "I'm not going to get back to Newport soon, am I?"

Xanthae gave her an apologetic look and a bit of a shrug. "To answer that, we first must decide how it is that you came to be in Prague. If you had to find yourself on such a mysterious journey, at least you have picked the best destination. Prague is the most beautiful city in all of Europe!" Xanthae beamed with pride, and Nevine could guess she was trying to put on a positive face for her.

Still, looking about at the exotic buildings and the castle walls up the hill, Nevine had to believe she might have been right about that. Prague seemed to be like something out of a fairy tale. She had come in for quite a shock in meeting the Ghoul of Vysehrad, but Xanthae seemed to be friendly enough. She was going to be in serious trouble once she got back to Grimoire Manor...but if it meant she was going on an adventure, perhaps it would be worth it.

They walked up the hill along several winding roads, and Nevine found herself getting slightly out of breath. They passed through a set of open gates that led through the thick walls of Vysehrad Castle and onto the grounds. As Xanthae had told her, there was no real castle left at Vysehrad other than the immense stone walls. The biggest building that Nevine could see was the Cathedral, which Xanthae told her was the Cathedral of Saint Paul and Peter. "Can't ever seem to have one without the other," Xanthae groused. The Basilica was surrounded on two sides by a cemetery, and Nevine was glad they did not get too close to that at night. There were several smaller buildings on the grounds, as well. It was toward one of these that they went.

Xanthae's observatory was a thirty-foot tall rectangular structure with a metal dome top that looked more or less how Nevine thought an observatory should. It sat on the south side of Vysehrad, furthest from the city, to be least affected by light coming from the street lamps. As such, the grounds here were so dark that the observatory itself would have been nearly invisible, had the dome not tended to reflect the light of the moon.

They trudged through the snow to the observatory's entrance. Xanthae produced a ring of keys and held the door open for Nevine. As they stepped inside, Xanthae reached out and pushed a large button. There was an audible pop and a hum, and a dozen or so naked light bulbs placed about the large room began to glow.

Xanthae closed the door behind them, then stood with her hands on her hips, beaming. "Ours is one of the first buildings in Prague to be fully electrified. We actually have an electric generator down the hill that uses the current of the Vltava River to produce energy. You are impressed, yes? When we have time, I will teach you how it works."

The bulbs didn't really throw off a lot of light, but it was enough to see the room they had entered was huge and impressive. Most noticeable was the huge telescope which pointed up at the top of the dome roof. For the moment, the dome was closed. Throughout the rest of the room were scattered many tables upon which rested numerous beakers, vials, racks of equipment, and machines of all sorts. On the walls, as in Grimoire Manor, were portraits of old people, although most of these looked smug as compared to the hostile portraits at Grimoire.

Several certificates adorned the walls, one for Xanthae's doctorate from Charles University, another denoting the patronage of the Emperor Franz Joseph. She also noticed a periodic table, although it seemed to be missing some of the elements. There was a young man wearing patched clothes and a top hat working at some of the machines. He was tall and thin, and gave Nevine a friendly smile when she walked in. He could have been handsome, Nevine thought, if only he had a haircut and some different clothes.

"Wow," Nevine said breathlessly, forgetting how afraid she had recently been. "This is a really neat place!"

Xanthae looked quite pleased. "This is where all the brilliant science is done. We also have several small bedrooms in the building, one of which can be yours until we figure out how to get you back to Rhode Island. We have a kitchen with a methane stove and full running water throughout the building." Xanthae pointed up toward the ceiling. "We have several rainwater collection units on the roof. Gravity, of course, pulls the water down through the building, stopped only by the traps in the faucets, bath and water closet. So I think you will see what we have all the comforts modern science can offer."

Nevine smiled politely, although she was unsure how a bunch of dim light bulbs and running water related to modern science.

"This tall fellow is my student Petyr Weiss." She introduced the young man in the top hat. Petyr put his fingers to the hat's brim in greetings, never losing his smile. "He is the son of a childhood friend of mine. Petyr, our guest is Miss Nevine Turner, an American who almost was devoured by the Ghoul." Nevine thought it curious that Petyr wore his top hat indoors, although the structure was quite chilly.

"I am glad to hear that you made good your escape, Miss Turner," he said, his accent much like that of his professor.

"Please call me Nevine. The teachers at Grimoire Manor call me Miss Turner and I don't like it very much."

"Nevine it is then." He bowed and clicked his heels together.

"Petyr, our guest is undoubtedly hungry. Would you be so kind as to prepare some beef goulash, perhaps with dumplings?"

"I shall fire up the methane burners at once," he replied, leaving his machines behind and moving off to the kitchens.

"He's a good fellow," Xanthae explained with a wink. "Brilliant, just like his mother. I'm quite fond of him, even if his father was German."

Xanthae led Nevine to a small room with a cot and a small table and chair. "This room has served as our guest room whenever visiting scientists use the telescope. We need to get you some spare clothing in case you may be with us for at least a short time. Let us go back into the main room. I check to see how Petyr is doing and perhaps we can speak a bit."

Nevine waited in the main room for a few minutes. Trying to be careful as she knew that she should, she nonetheless explored the variety of machines that lay about the room in no obvious arrangement. Her gaze landed on one, sitting on a big table, which seemed to consist mainly of one large metal ball next to a smaller one, both of them on long tubes. There was a hand-crank at the base. Giving into temptation, Nevine began to spin the crank, and as she did so felt something move around inside of the tube supporting the larger ball. After a few seconds, she noticed a slight tingling sensation on her skin and the hair on her arms seemed to be standing on end. Curious, she continued spinning the crank. At last, there was a loud pop as an arc of purple flame jumped from between the large and small metal balls. Nevine cried out in surprise and jumped back from the contraption.

"Ah," said Xanthae, reentering the room with Petyr behind her, "I see that you have found my electrostatic generator. Quite harmless, although perhaps best in the future to ask what something does before you blast your fingers off." Xanthae carried a big bowl of goulash, while Petyr had a beaker filled with water, plates, and wooden cups for them all. They found a relatively clear table and settled down to eat.

"How does it work?" Nevine asked once she had a few bites of delicious hot goulash in her stomach.

"The generator?" Xanthae said, clearly pleased that Nevine had asked. "It uses friction. You have noticed that on a cold day, if you rub your feet on a rug, then touch something metal, you may get a zap of electricity?"

Nevine nodded and smiled mischievously. "It's more fun if you zap someone else!"

"Yes, well, the generator works more or less like that. There is a strip of silk in the bigger tube around two rollers. You crank the handle and the silk strip brushes against metal fibers at the bottom of the machine. This makes static electricity kind of like rubbing your feet on a rug on a cold day makes static electricity. This electricity attaches to the silk strip, which as you crank it, moves the electricity up to a second metal brush at the top of the big ball." With this, she reached out and rapped her knuckles against the big steel ball, producing a clanging sound. "The electric charge transfers to the brush, called an electrode, which transfers the charge to the outside of the metal sphere.

41

As the charge builds up on the larger ball, it must be discharged, so it leaps across to the smaller ball, which allows it to escape into the ground."

"Is that like how lighting works?"

"More or less." Xanthae nodded. "As the storm clouds move, they experience friction, which builds up static electricity. The charge builds up and it wants to discharge into the ground so it will leap across to a tall object, just like the spark crossed the spark gap on the machine you found."

"And thunder, then, is just like the pop I heard when I made the spark on your machine!" Nevine realized.

Petyr nodded. "The professor is never going to stop talking tonight if you get her going like this."

"Wow, that's kind of neat," Nevine said. "It looks like magic."

Xanthae smiled, although her voice was stern, "Well, it's not. It's science. Magic is either for charlatans or," —and now she lowered her voice— "or those foolish enough to consort with devils or demons in exchange for unnatural abilities."

"You will have to pardon Professor Halruaa," Petyr said, his mouth full of goulash. "She tends to get a bit dramatic. I'm sure that she's rattled off all her accomplishments to you already, but I suspect she's neglected to mention she has the emotional control of a wolverine and the common sense of a fruit fly."

Xanthae looked ready to stab the young man. "It would explain my rash decision in taking you on, wouldn't it?"

"Even a child stumbling in the dark finds gold sometimes." Petyr smirked.

Xanthae ignored him. "The Ghoul of Vysehrad is just one such example. We have been trying to hunt him down for weeks now, without much success."

"Is he human?"

"Once," replied Xanthae, with a touch of sadness in her voice. "Although we believe that he has risen from the dead through some form of dark magic. He must feed on the living in order to stay alive...if his state can be called living. We don't yet know who or what is responsible for bringing him back from the dead."

"Like a vampire, then?"

Xanthae nodded. "In some ways. Perhaps neither so charming nor attractive as a vampire is said to be. A ghoul rarely speaks, and carries the stench of the grave. He feeds on the energy of the living, and leaves his victims as withered corpses; themselves to rise as ghouls. We have been fortunate so far in tracking down the Ghoul's victims before they spread his unholy affliction any further. We have had no luck stopping the Ghoul himself, though. Tonight was the first time that I lay eyes upon him."

"Found you the ghoul?" Petyr cried out.

"She saved my life!" Nevine exclaimed.

Xanthae waved them both off. "Yes, yes, we saw the ghoul, but he got away. We have learned," she explained to Nevine, "that the ghoul and his spawn may be frightened of gunshots, but are not injured by them like living people. Only fire seems to kill them."

Nevine wrinkled her nose at the unpleasant thought.

"In here we are safe, though," she assured Nevine. "There will be enough time to worry about the Ghoul tomorrow. We'll also have to consider how to get you back to Rhode Island. In case it should be that you are not able to leave immediately, I think that Petyr and I should begin teaching you a few words of Czech. Not so many people speak English, and there are some important phrases you should know…hello, thank you, please…"

"'Where's the water closet?'" Petyr chimed in, "and 'could I have more goulash please'? Actually, that last bit sounds like a good idea." He helped himself to another bowl of the goulash.

"You look tired," Xanthae said, and it was true. Nevine felt as if she had been awake for a long and hard day. "Let's get you settled away. We can think of what we need to do in the morning."

A few minutes later, tucked away in yet another strange room, Nevine reflected on the odd and unusual turns that her life had taken over the past day. First the ghost of Grimoire Manor, and now the Ghoul of Vysehrad. She didn't know what to think of it all, and didn't even know where she might wake up once she had gone to sleep! What was happening to her simply didn't make sense, yet she had to admit that it was an adventure, and she had been lucky enough to find Xanthae and Petyr. She wondered when she woke up, if she would find herself back at Grimoire Manor or in yet another strange place. Well, there was only one way to find that out.

Chapter 4

The Ghoul of Vysehrad

There was a little window in Nevine's observatory bedroom, and she awoke to see fresh sunlight gleaming in through layers of frost. She sat up and stretched. She was still in Prague…so it hadn't all been a dream. This realization evoked conflicting feelings. She didn't much like Grimoire Manor, but she was going to miss her friend Aurora. Nevine wondered what the others were going to think when they woke up to find her missing.

Nevine found Xanthae in the main observatory room, looking through a heavy book, and eating lazily from a plate of eggs. "Ah, good morning to you, Nevine," Xanthae greeted. "It is good to have you awake. Please have some breakfast. Petyr is out on an errand, but we have much to discuss. I'll teach you a few simple Czech words that you will need, then we'll get you some clothes. While we are out, we can decide how best to return you to Rhode Island."

"I've been thinking about that," Nevine said, "and if it were possible, I wouldn't mind staying here for a little while."

Xanthae seemed surprised. "You don't like this Grimoire Manor very much, then?"

Nevine shook her head. "No, I don't like it at all. The teachers are not very nice, except for Ms. Emily. I had one friend, Aurora, and if it were possible, I'd rather find a way to bring her here, rather than go back. Perhaps I could help you chase the Ghoul?"

"Such things are very dangerous, as you saw yourself last night. I would not want to…" She seemed to search for the right word for a moment. "…kidnap you when there are others who may be worried about you." Xanthae's expression softened. "Let me think on it. Perhaps the day will make things clearer for us both."

After breakfast, Nevine put on her coats and joined Xanthae walking down the Vysehrad hill back into the city of Prague. The sun was out, and it was a beautiful day, although the temperature was surprisingly cold. A crunchy layer of snow covered the ground and Nevine had to be careful not to slip, particularly when walking down the steep hill away from the castle. There were a fair number of people out now, dressed oddly, like in movies she had seen of *The Christmas Carol*. A few rode horses, and occasionally she saw a cart or stagecoach go by, but there were no automobiles. Nevine remarked on this to Xanthae.

"Well," Xanthae said, laughing, "automobiles are very rare and expensive. Most people cannot afford to buy one."

"Wow," Nevine said, her eyes wide, "I had heard that other countries were behind the times, but I never imagined how much!"

"What you are talking about?" Xanthae asked in dismay. "Prague is certainly as advanced as your American farming villages!" She got a slightly haughty tone to her voice.

"We don't live on farms anymore. And everyone

has a car. Well, I don't, but I will when I get out of college."

Xanthae stopped walking suddenly, and Nevine kept going a few steps before she noticed it. When she turned back, Xanthae had a curious expression on her face. "What is it, Professor Halruaa?"

"Nevine," she began, her voice very serious indeed, "could you tell me what year is it?"

"Well, that's easy," Nevine replied and recited the day, the year, and who was the current president.

Xanthae got a funny look in her eye. "Well, I think we can stop worrying about sending you back to Rhode Island then."

Nevine didn't mind the sound of that, but she was curious. "Why do you say that?"

"In addition to jumping continents, you appear to have jumped centuries. Today is actually the first of December, 1888." She paused to take in Nevine's reaction.

"Well, that does explain the funny clothes and all the horses," Nevine said, although inwardly she was quite shocked. More and more, she was confused as to what was happening. How could she have traveled, not only so far, but also backward through time? None of this was making any sense. She looked at Xanthae, who was regarding her very closely, "You do believe me, don't you?"

Xanthae thought for a moment. "I don't believe that you are lying to me, and I see no evidence in your behavior that you are mad. Still, I have never seen any evidence that time travel is remotely possible. I have no explanation for it, which troubles me."

"But you hunt ghosts, don't you? You must be

used to the supernatural?"

Xanthae shook her head. "I do hunt ghosts, but you must realize one thing. If something exists, it is not supernatural. What we call supernatural are only those things which we cannot explain. I don't believe God would create these beautiful laws of nature only to immediately begin breaking them." She smiled. "Yet your point is well taken. I don't have a good explanation for ghosts or, indeed, ghouls either. I have theories, but theories are only useful if they are testable, and I haven't had enough opportunities for that yet as it pertains to ghosts or ghouls. Unfortunately, without a testable theory about what brought you to this time, I have no way of sending you back."

Nevine smiled a little at that, although part of her felt very sad at the thought of never seeing Aurora again.

Xanthae patted Nevine's shoulder as if to comfort her. "You can stay with Petyr and me then until we figure things out. We'll need to work hard to teach you Czech and I'll expect you to do your share around the observatory as well. There are many things in that building that are not intended for visitors, so I will have to teach you to use them safely."

Nevine nodded. "Oh, yes, I would like that!"

"Tonight," Xanthae said, "Petyr and I have been invited to a recital of Dvorak's latest works at the Church of Our Lady in Front of Tyn. You'll come along as well, and we'll have to find you a suitable dress. Mind you, I don't have much money, but we'll get you the prettiest dress that I can."

"Dvorak?" Nevine wrinkled her nose, thinking. "Is that a punk band?"

Xanthae looked at Nevine for a moment before saying, "Truly, I have no idea how to answer your question."

****

That evening found Nevine wearing the prettiest dress she had ever seen—light blue and made out of silk and lace. Petyr was dressed in a black suit with his top hat, and even Xanthae had found a lovely red dress to wear, although her hair was still wild and she didn't wear any makeup. Nevine decided Petyr looked rather dashing in a tall, lanky kind of way. Xanthae also took the step of hiring a small coach for the night, to save them the long walk from Vysehrad to the Church of Our Lady in Front of Tyn on the cold December evening. It was a gesture that Nevine suspected Xanthae could ill afford.

Although not a church night, the cathedral was packed with people, most of them quite old and well-dressed. The youngest adults were those outside examining the invitation cards, and they looked to be some kind of employees. There seemed to be very few children, and these were in tow of adults who kept them well controlled. A few people came up to speak with Xanthae, who always took pains to introduce Nevine and Petyr, although Nevine could not understand most of the conversations, as they were in that funny language. The cathedral itself was quite beautiful with huge pillars and beautiful stain glass. There also were people's names engraved along the side and near to some of the pillars. Xanthae explained to her that these were grave markers, and prominent people of Prague were sometimes buried right on the inside of the cathedrals. Nevine got shivers thinking that she was walking on dead people.

At last, they settled down in their seats in the church pews and waited for the recital to begin. If nothing else, it was reasonably warm in the cathedral. Nevine was becoming used to being cold all the time.

After a few moments, several old men walked out into the front of the church. Each was impeccably dressed, held an instrument such as a violin or viola, and neglected to smile at or otherwise acknowledge the audience. A hush fell over the crowd.

Dubiously, Nevine looked up at Xanthae and whispered, "Are you sure that I'm going to like this music?"

Xanthae smiled at Nevine and whispered back, "Dvorak is one of the finest modern composers. Believe me, your mind is going to be…" she struggled for the word, "…entranced!"

Ten minutes later, Nevine had her head in Xanthae's lap, fast asleep. Only in the most distant sense was Nevine aware of Xanthae lovingly stroking her hair while she slept. Occasionally, a particularly loud note might cause her to stir, but otherwise, she was unable to be roused.

It was only a sudden commotion in the church that finally caused Nevine to wake and look about. The commotion was caused by a simply dressed man, shouting and calling out. Nevine couldn't understand him, but from the looks and gasps from the rest of the crowd, Nevine could guess that it was serious. The musicians stopped playing as all attention was on him. At last, there was a part of his urgent calls that even she could understand.

"Doktor Halruaa!" he called out, and soon all eyes

were on Xanthae.

Xanthae stood, and the man spoke with her rapidly and urgently. After hearing what the man had said, Xanthae grabbed Nevine's hand and pulled her from the church, with Petyr following behind. Once they were outside, she explained to Nevine, "The Ghoul has struck tonight. A woman has been killed and I must attend to the scene."

"Oh no," Nevine exclaimed, thinking how easily it could have been her the night before.

"I should have known," Xanthae was mumbling to herself, although she was still using English, "when he was unsuccessful last night, he would strike again tonight."

"Where has he killed the woman?" Petyr asked. Even though he had the longest legs of the three of them, even he was struggling to keep up with Xanthae's furious pace. For her part, Nevine was practically running beside her new benefactor as they made their way back to the street in search of their coach. Behind them, a small group followed; the man who had summoned Xanthae as well as some of the people who had attended the recital. Nevine could see that people were going to edge toward panic as the Ghoul continued to strike.

"He has struck," said Xanthae, not looking back at her student, "near to the town hall."

"He's moving further north, further Vysehrad!" Petyr reasoned aloud.

They were back to their rented coach by then, and Xanthae set about organizing the three of them. "Petyr, do you have any of the flares?"

He smiled a big affable smile. "Of course,

Professor Halruaa! I always bring a few along. You never know when they may be useful." He winked at Nevine.

Xanthae took two of the flares from Petyr and handed one of them to Nevine. The thing felt heavy in her hand and she was somewhat surprised to be trusted with it. "Nevine, the Ghoul does not like bright light. As you saw yourself last night, it bothers him more than a pistol shot. I don't believe that he can see in such bright light. If you find yourself in any danger, pull on this metal cap." She indicated the metal cover on the flare. "The removed cap will expose the little bit of phosphorous in the flare to oxygen in the air, which will ignite it, in turn causing the magnesium fuel to burn. You must be warned—magnesium burns very hot when ignited and you must be very careful not to let it touch your skin or clothes. Use the flare only if you are threatened by the Ghoul or his spawn."

Nevine held the flare with great care in her hands. She felt honored to be trusted with such a dangerous implement. "I will be very careful," she said. "I want to be able to help you."

Petyr looked a little less sure and said to Nevine, "If you must ignite it, hold it away from your body." He turned to Xanthae and asked, "Perhaps it would be best to drop Nevine off someplace safe?" Nevine was a bit insulted at his tone, as if she were just a child.

Xanthae patted Petyr on the shoulder and said, "Between here and the observatory there is no place I would consider safe, and we haven't time to return to the observatory." She winked at Nevine and gave her the first smile that Xanthae had allowed herself since learning of the Ghoul's attack. "Besides, if Nevine wishes to stay with ghost-hunters, she'll need to learn the craft. I should remind you, Petyr, that you were the same age as Nevine the first time I took you out on a hunt."

"Yes," Petyr said with a frown, "and I still have the scar on my—"

"And never will you let me forget it, will you?" Xanthae demanded.

A few minutes later, the coach stopped in the shadow of the Town Hall Tower and they all climbed down, Xanthae with her four-barreled pistol ready, Petyr and Nevine each with flares. Other coaches had followed them from the church, and quickly they had a renewed throng of townspeople following them to the scene of the attack. It was not difficult to find as, not surprisingly, a small crowd had gathered there as well, their lanterns bobbing and their talk quite animated.

As instructed, Nevine stayed behind Xanthae as she pushed her way through the crowd to the scene of the death. There Nevine saw her first dead person. The woman had been tall, almost six feet, and was still dressed in an elegant dress with a shawl over her shoulders. Her long blond hair splayed over the cobblestones of the street. Aside from that, it was difficult to believe she had been alive just an hour previously. There was little left of her but a skeleton with skin drawn tightly over it. She looked as if all the water had been sucked out of her. Every last bit of life essence drained away. Her eye sockets were hollow, dark pits that stared out randomly, and her jaw hung open like a skull's. She looked much like pictures of unwrapped mummies Nevine had seen in science books. It seemed so unreal until she realized that this was the fate she had so narrowly avoided the night before.

"Quickly, I need kerosene!" Xanthae said, then seemed to remember herself and repeated the demand in Czech to the assembled crowd. Several of the men ran into nearby buildings, presumably at her behest.

Petyr put his body between Nevine and the dead woman. He looked back and reminded her, "We must act quickly before the victim's body has the chance to return herself as a ghoul. The only way to be sure she is dead for good is to use—"

"Fire," Nevine completed the sentence for him. She was watching the woman's body as he spoke to her and so she was the first to see the body twitch, just a few fingers at first, then the woman's entire left arm.

A frightened murmur spread across the assembled crowd, and the entire group took several instinctive steps back from the body. A woman screamed and several people crossed themselves.

The dead woman pushed herself off the ground into a kneeling position, her dark eyeless sockets looking over the crowd assembled around her. Her arms were little more than bone and sinew, but they seemed to possess an unnatural strength. Her jaw clicked shut, then opened again, and she made a sound like a sigh as her dead lungs expelled what had been her final breath. Although her face could make no expression, it was impossible not to feel rage radiating from her as she looked over the assembled mass.

One young man stepped forward with tears in his eyes and held out his hand toward the ghoul woman. He spoke to her, weeping soothingly in Czech, and Nevine guessed that he must have been her husband.

"No!" Xanthae cried out to the young man, but she was too far away to intervene. Like a snake, the ghoul woman reached out with one of her now clawed hands for the man who had once been her husband. The man cried out in shock and pain as her talons raked across his arm. The ghoul stumbled to her feet, intent on seizing the man into a deadly embrace.

It was Petyr who leapt between them, igniting his flare. The ghoul woman shrunk back from it, releasing her grip on her husband. Several bystanders grabbed the wounded man and yanked him back to safety. Many in the crowd had run by now, but some had stayed, intent on helping perhaps, or simply unable to tear their eyes away from the scene unfolding before them in the lurid red light of the flare.

"Petyr," Xanthae called, "do not get so close. Ghouls are cunning. And where is that kerosene!" She was trying to aim her pistol, but Petyr was now between her and the skeletal woman.

The ghoul crouched and made another odd sighing sound, its eyeless skull intent on Petyr, the man who had robbed her of her prey. Petyr was too close, too near to the ghoul's talons, as Nevine could see, and placed himself at great risk.

Now the ghoul leapt, reaching out and under the glowing flare. Her talons caught beneath Petyr's knee and she pulled his leg out from underneath him. He toppled backward into the street, nearly hitting his head against the curb. His flare went spinning out of his hand, landing down the street where it rolled away, now useless. Petyr crawled backward a few inches, eager to get away from the ghoul.

A deafening shot rang out as Xanthae fired her

pistol into the creature. The ghoul stumbled backward a pace before turning her orbless eyes on Xanthae in fury. Xanthae fired again, and Nevine could see the shots did little harm, but they did distract the ghoul while Petyr managed to scramble to safety. As for herself, Xanthae was now alone, the crowd having driven far back and away from her, and she was now the focus of the ghoul's wrath. She fired a third time and then a fourth, the last bullet nearly knocking the ghoul over. Then, her pistol was empty, and she now stood there defenseless as the creature sighed its deathly breath and advanced on her, intent on sucking her life energy from her.

Without thinking, Nevine ran between them, blocking the ghoul's path. Hoping that she had understood what Xanthae had told her to do, she pulled the cap off her flare and was rewarded with a bright green glow as the flare hissed to life. She held it above her and was relieved to see the ghoul shrink back away from it. Sparks from the flare rained down on her hand and burned the skin, but she ignored it. She was not going to let harm come to the woman who had saved her life.

Several of the men who had gone in search of kerosene now came running back with canisters of the flammable fluid. Xanthae shouted out orders to the men in Czech. They clearly were reluctant to follow those orders, and ultimately it was Petyr who snatched one of the metal canisters from them and again approached the ghoul close enough to splash her with the fluid. It was dangerous work, as the ghoul tried to lash out at him again, but he had learned not to get too close and Nevine kept her at bay with her flare.

At last, the ghoul was reasonably doused and

Xanthae shouted, "Nevine, your flare, use your flare!" Hoping the softball team one of her foster parents had made her join was going to pay off now, Nevine lobbed the flare at the ghoul woman, hoping to time it so that it was the burning end that contacted her. Nevine held her breath, watching the burning green tip go end over end until the tip landed just as she hoped it would against the side of the ghoul's dress.

The ghoul didn't immediately burst into flame as Nevine had expected, but the kerosene caught more slowly. Desperately, the ghoul tried to beat out the first flames, but this only succeeded in getting the burning liquid on her hands and arms. The ghoul didn't scream—it apparently could make no sound other than those soft sighs, but it ran, confused and purposeless, into the street. All of her was burning now, from head to toe, the flames cackling in the cold night air and sending embers into the air. What was left of the crowd parted away from her, and she bumped up against a street lamp, then a cart before she fell and silently came to rest in the center of the street.

There were men with buckets of water now, throwing water on the roofs of the nearby buildings to keep the embers from starting fires. Nevine saw Xanthae give them instructions; apparently to let the body burn, to be sure that it was finally dead for good.

Petyr came over to Nevine and put his arm around her shoulder. "You are all right?"

Nevine nodded, although she wasn't entirely sure. Her heart was still racing very fast and her brain was still trying to make sense of everything she had seen…and done. Petyr kept his arm around her while she sucked in several deep breaths.

A minute later, Xanthae allowed the crowd to extinguish the flames that engulfed what remained of the ghoul woman. She then stood beside Nevine with both admiration and concern in her eyes. "Are you not hurt?" she asked tenderly.

Nevine shook her head. "I'm fine," she said, then a second time more confidently, "I'm fine."

"You were very brave," Xanthae said with a smile. "You saved my life."

"That wasn't the same ghoul that attacked me last night," Nevine said, her teeth chattering a bit.

"No," Petyr replied. "This poor woman was merely one of his victims. We have been fortunate so far in tracking down all of the Vysehrad Ghoul's spawn before they could spread this...affliction further. The Vyserhrad Ghoul himself has proven to be more cunning, more elusive than his spawn."

"She would have escaped as well had not men in the crowd kept kerosene for their lamps." Xanthae looked thoughtfully between Petyr and Nevine. "We were poorly prepared tonight and should discuss how to be better equipped in the future."

Petyr nodded and then looked at Nevine. "Well, this is what we do," he said, "between gazing and the stars and planets and developing important scientific theorems..."

"...and for some of us napping and playing at games." Xanthae nudged Petyr. She looked at Nevine with a thoughtful expression. "You'd be well advised to find a different mentor who can keep you in better safety than I can. Yet tonight you've earned a place among us if you wish it." She extended her hand to Nevine, palm up.

Nevine thought for a moment, although there never really was any doubt as to her choice. With a smile, she took Xanthae's hand and gave it a squeeze.

Chapter 5

The Mayoress

Despite the frightening things she had witnessed that night, Nevine felt strangely exhilarated as they rode home in their coach. She was proud of herself for helping Xanthae and Petyr fight the ghoul spawn, and basked in the praise Xanthae had given her. It seemed like such a long time since any adult had taken pride in her. She was beginning to feel as if she had been brought to Prague for a reason.

"So you see our problem," Petyr was saying, gnawing on a piece of cured meat one of the local shopkeepers had given out to the ghost hunters of Prague. It wasn't exactly money or a medal, but they were all hungry and it would do. "Fire is the best way of destroying the ghoul spawn that we have found, yet we don't have a good way of delivering the fire. We can't exactly walk around with kerosene canisters, they're too heavy, and you have to get very close to the ghouls to splash them, which is dangerous."

Xanthae added, "The only other option we have considered is glass vials of kerosene that could be hurled like grenades. To be accurate, though, they wouldn't be able to hold very much kerosene, otherwise they'd get too heavy and we have the same problem as with the metal canisters. I should mention that kerosene is very dangerous. Many people are burned seriously by it each year using it in cooking fires. I don't want to see you near it, Nevine, without my direction. I don't yet even trust Petyr with it."

Petyr nodded, chewing on his cured beef. "With good reason," he agreed.

Nevine listened with interest. Finally, a thought came to her. "What about a flamethrower?"

"A what?" Xanthae and Petyr said at the same time, eyebrows raised.

"I don't know how they work," Nevine admitted, "but I had to watch a documentary on World War II…long story…but I remember these soldiers wearing them. A flamethrower is like a gun, except the soldier wears a big tank on his back, and the gun spits flame."

Xanthae and Petyr looked at each other for a moment thoughtfully. After a moment, Xanthae said, "We could conceivably use a compressed inert gas to propel the kerosene."

Petyr looked excited. "We could hook a methane burner under the nozzle to ignite the kerosene. I can try putting some parts together, come up with a working model. We have a week to work on it since the Vysehrad Ghoul only feeds once a week."

"Nevine," Xanthae said with an appreciative smile, "I think you may very well be a genius." Her eyes twinkled with excitement.

Nevine beamed. "It's what I do."

That evening they dined on chicken in sauce (care of Petyr's cooking once again) and apple strudel. Exhausted, she practically fell into bed and was asleep in no time at all.

****

She awoke to the sound of shouting outside in the main observatory. It was morning, although she barely took notice of this, rushing to the door to see what the matter was. There were two soldiers in the main room, in white jackets and black caps. The older of the two was perhaps fifty years of age, with the younger in his thirties. They were very precise in their appearance and professional in their demeanor. They stood calmly by the main door while Xanthae shouted and all but spat in their faces. She was speaking rapidly in Czech, so Nevine could not understand what had upset her so much, but it worried her to see Xanthae so angered. Petyr was behind Xanthae, attempting to calm her down. The soldiers did not appear upset by Xanthae's anger, but maintained an air of arrogant disinterest.

Feeling concerned, Nevine approached Petyr and tapped on his shoulder to get his attention. He turned to her, his concerned expression filled with worry.

"Petyr," she asked as Xanthae drowned out their conversation with more curses in Czech, "what's going on?"

For a moment, he looked as if he struggled to think of what to say. "It seems that word of our activities yesterday evening have made their way around the city, as we might have expected them to. Some people were apparently surprised to learn we had with us a new student in the personage of yourself. These gentlemen," —he gestured toward the soldiers— "have themselves been hunting the Vysehrad Ghoul. Now, however, they have come to take you before the Mayoress of Prague, who would like to ask you some questions."

Nevine didn't like the sound of that. "Am I in some kind of trouble?"

"No," Petyr replied, trying to sound comforting. "I think the mayoress is just..." He struggled for words again.

"The mayoress," Xanthae cut in, her eyes wide and angry, "is a sinister, power-hungry, unscrupulous woman who enjoys sticking her nose in business that is not hers just to remind people that she can. She is the worst kind of vicious, untrustworthy sort of person...a politician to the core!"

"Eh," said the older soldier, almost looking embarrassed, "I should mention...I do speak English." He seemed to be trying to calm matters down, although Nevine could see the younger soldier becoming more and more agitated.

"I care not!" cried Xanthae, rounding on him. "I will curse the mayoress in English or Czech, or German or Latin...or...let's see, what other languages do I speak?"

"Professor Halruaa, as you may now suspect, does not entirely trust the mayoress," Petyr explained with an apologetic look. "An impression made worse because these soldiers will not let us accompany you."

"I see," Nevine said. It was a frightening thought to wonder why this woman, the mayoress, who Xanthae clearly did not like, would want to speak with her. Why would she want to speak to a teenage girl? And she understood why Xanthae was angry. It did sound sinister that her new friends were not allowed to accompany her. But she could see also Xanthae's anger was only delaying the inevitable, and she didn't want to become a source of trouble for Xanthae.

"Professor Halruaa," said the younger soldier, his face becoming red as Xanthae's anger began to infect him, "I'll remind you that speaking out in such a manner against the Emperor's agents could be considered sedition. If you don't control yourself, I'll be forced to arrest you." Nevine's heart raced when she heard these words.

Xanthae was only provoked further by his words and looked ready to round on the soldier before Nevine spoke up. "I'll go," she said simply. She was as frightened as she had ever been in her life.

All eyes were on her for a moment, each of them looking rather shocked. "You mustn't," Xanthae said at last, rushing to her protectively. "You don't understand what this woman is capable of."

Nevine held her benefactor's hand and gave it a reassuring squeeze. "I don't want to get you in trouble, professor. Besides, if the mayoress isn't very nice, I'm kind of used to that from adults. Even if she doesn't let me stay with you..." As she said this, she saw Xanthae's expression change from anger to something more like sadness...and fear. "...you and Petyr have treated me more kindly than anyone else I can remember."

Xanthae looked sad, almost defeated, and she squeezed Nevine's hand back. Nevine turned to the older of the two soldiers. "I'm ready to leave with you." The older soldier nodded, and Xanthae and Petyr watched as she left with him and his comrade. They had come in a cart, and the older soldier, whose name was Novak, helped her up onto the cart before sitting next to her. The younger soldier, whose name she was to learn was Skounic, climbed to the front of the cart and took the reins.

On the journey to the town hall, Novak spoke with

her kindly, although Nevine guessed he was quietly pumping her for information. He seemed to be most interested in the progress they had made in tracking the Ghoul of Vysehrad. Like Xanthae and Petyr, he said that he did not know where the Ghoul had come from but that he and Skounic were intent on catching and destroying the monster. Nevine was careful not to say too much to Novak, despite his kindness.

Soon they were at the town hall, not far from where they had fought the ghoul's spawn just the night before. The town hall was much more remarkable during the day, with a tall medieval-looking tower shadowing the buildings below. Novak and Skounic guided her inside the old-looking building and up several flights of stairs. There were other people in the hall, bureaucrats mostly, who regarded her either suspiciously or with indifference. She felt like she was back at Grimoire Manor, and missed the comfort she had felt at the observatory.

At last, she was brought to a large office. This room was well decorated with paintings, shelves of books, a suit of armor, and a huge globe on a pedestal. A long window looked out over the city below and a dark wooden desk blocked visitors away from the office's sole occupant. She was a woman in her thirties with long golden hair, dressed in an elegant gray dress. She was remarkably beautiful, but unlike Xanthae's beauty, which was wild and untamed, this woman was elegant and pristine, as if she had been sculpted from stone. Everything on her was perfectly in its place, as if the distance between the curls of her hair were carefully measured and placed. She had none of Xanthae's warmth. Indeed, the room around her seemed to be bereft altogether of heat, as if she drew the life of others into her own body. Nevine unconsciously shivered.

Novak and Skounic showed the woman great deference, not looking her in the eye, and Novak's fatherly warmth toward Nevine evaporated. The woman dismissed the two soldiers with a little wave and beckoned Nevine to sit in a stiff wooden chair with a similar flick of her hand.

The woman stared at Nevine for a few seconds, studying her. "So, Nevine Turner," she said at last, her voice unfriendly and heavily accented, "I understand you are American."

Nevine was surprised the woman already knew so much about her. She had only told Xanthae and Petyr about her background and she doubted they had spoken about it with the mayoress, given Xanthae's reaction this morning. Nevine nodded.

"How," the mayoress asked, "did you come to be in Prague?"

Nevine was instantly on the defensive. She had a feeling answering the question with the complete truth, as she had with Xanthae, was going to be dangerous. If nothing else, the mayoress might use the truth to say that Nevine was crazy as a way to separate her from Xanthae. On the other hand, the mayoress already seemed to be a person who was not easily fooled, and Nevine was wary of trying an outright lie. So she aimed for something in the middle: using the truth, but only portions of it. "Well," Nevine said, trying to appear confident about her answer, "I've never had a real family. I've been moved all around from one family to another until I was lucky enough to meet Professor Halruaa, and she said I could stay with her." She gulped, hoping that was enough.

The mayoress regarded her coldly, then grinned a little, although it was a grin that gave Nevine shivers. She would never have guessed that so pretty a woman could be so frightening. "Very touching," she said without emotion. "I particularly enjoyed how you answered my question without giving any details of how an American orphan ended up in the Austro-Hungarian Empire." The mayoress had stood and paced a bit while she talked; now she stopped and stared at Nevine once again.

Nevine gulped and said nothing, not trusting herself to say anything that wouldn't give too much away.

"Fine," the mayoress said at last. "We're each entitled to our secrets. I should inform you of one thing, though. You must understand that as Mayoress of Prague, I am the emperor's direct magistrate in this city and I wield his authority to see to the safety of its inhabitants. One could argue that the safety of young girls is not ensured by the company of kerosene-hurling ghost-chasing people such as Professor Halruaa." She eyed Nevine with interest, awaiting her response.

Nevine knew she couldn't always succeed with silence. Fortunately, a thought from her history classes came to her. "Isn't it true," she began, forcing her voice to rise above the timidity that she felt, "that children and young women work in a lot of dangerous places like mines or factories where their fingers or hands can get chopped off? I don't think I'm in any more danger than those children, and if I can help Professor Halruaa find the Ghoul of Vysehrad, aren't I helping others in the city stay safe?"

The mayoress looked thoughtful. "That," she said, a burning ember of new interest flickering in her eye, "was a very good response. You're a very clever young lady, I would wager, and I'd guess being without parents for so long has forced you to be resourceful." She came around the desk and sat on its edge, so she towered over Nevine in her uncomfortable wooden chair. "You'd like to settle down now, though, wouldn't you? Perhaps you'd like to stay with Professor Halruaa…make her…your mother?"

Nevine gulped again. "I'd like to stay with the professor, yes."

"You know, I have a certain fondness for Professor Halruaa. We are alike in many ways. Both of us are women of accomplishment in the world of men. Do you know what it takes for a woman to succeed in this empire?"

Nevine shook her head.

The mayoress stood again, walking away, back behind her desk. "You'll learn soon enough, then. Professor Halruaa will make a fine tutor for you. Yet there will be many who would take delight in watching you fail, if only because you are a girl."

"I'll take my chances," Nevine said defiantly.

"Very well then." The mayoress sounded pleased. "I will consent to officially designate Professor Halruaa as your guardian under two conditions to which you must agree."

Nevine's heart lifted at the thought that Xanthae would officially be recognized as her caregiver, enforced by the woman Nevine thought might have taken her away from Xanthae. "Yes, I'll do anything."

The mayoress smiled, and Nevine's heart chilled as

she saw the mockery in that smile. "Such a sweet young lady you are, Nevine. The first is that I would like for you to pass along a simple message to your professor. The two gentlemen, Novak and Skounic, who escorted you here today, have been tasked by me with the same purpose Professor Halruaa has taken upon herself, namely the location and destruction of the Ghoul of Vysehrad. In order to quicken things, I will offer a bounty to whichever group is successful in this task, either the professor's little group or Novak and Skounic. In the event of…as they say in America, a 'tie'…the bounty shall be null and void. The bounty shall go to one group, but not both."

"But," ventured Nevine, feeling confused, "wouldn't it be better if we could cooperate with the two soldiers?"

The mayoress sighed with a flicker of impatience. "Asking questions was not part of the arrangement I had offered you. You are to take the message to Professor Halruaa, or I will have to reconsider my generosity."

"Okay," Nevine agreed, "I'll tell her."

"Second, I am planning a masquerade ball five days from today in honor of the emperor who will be in Prague. I have an official invitation here for you." She passed a thick perfumed envelope to Nevine. "Naturally, your attendance, along with that of Professor Halruaa, will be expected as part of our arrangements. I will pass along official documentation assigning your guardianship to Professor Halruaa at that time."

Nevine picked up the envelope and held it tightly, fearing it might somehow be unexpectedly lost on her way back to the observatory.

"There is one last thing, not a condition, merely a gift to a young girl with such promise." From the desk, the mayoress produced a little diamond pendant on a gold chain. She walked from behind the desk and put the chain around Nevine's neck. Nevine was so surprised she barely remembered to hold her hair up so that the mayoress could clasp the chain behind her neck. The diamond was not terribly big, nor the chain very thick, but the necklace was pretty nonetheless, and the only thing of real value she had ever owned. Given the mayoress' manner toward her, she was quite taken aback by the gift and unsure of what to think of it.

"Thank you," Nevine managed to say, still in shock. "It's beautiful."

"It is a sign of my favor and will be recognized as such by those in my service," the mayoress told her, admiring the little gem as it dangled from Nevine's neck. "Now we are done for today. I'll expect to see you in five evenings, seventh of December, do not forget. Good day." And with that, the mayoress returned to her desk and her paperwork. It was as if Nevine had suddenly become invisible to her.

"Good day," Nevine repeated timidly and wasn't sure if she was heard. Feeling unsure, she let herself out the door and found Novak waiting on the other side.

"How did your interview go?" he asked, as he led her back outside to the cart.

"I'm not sure," Nevine said honestly.

"Then it went very well," he said cryptically.

****

"That arrogant, sinister, meddlesome woman!" Xanthae was shouting, and then shifted back into

Czech. From the way Petyr winced, Nevine guessed she was missing some choice words. Nevine was back at the observatory, and Novak and Skounic were gone. Xanthae had been delighted to see Nevine back safely, but when Nevine had passed the message about the bounty for the Ghoul along, Xanthae had not been pleased.

"She does this," Xanthae said when she finally calmed down enough to remember her English again, "for the simple amusement of it. She wants to watch us and those two bumbling soldiers go stumbling over each other to get her bounty. Well, we don't need her money." Petyr raised his eyebrows at this as if it were news to him. "And if Novak and Skounic manage to destroy the Ghoul before us, so much the better. All that is important is that the people of this city are safe."

"But," Petyr said timidly, tugging at a hole in his jacket as if it were an unconscious gesture, "if we were to beat Novak and Skounic to the Ghoul, we wouldn't turn down the bounty, would we?"

Xanthae frowned. "Now see, that's just the kind of thinking the mayoress wants us to indulge in. Soon we'll start focusing on speed rather than good planning, take unnecessary chances that could get us killed. My stipend will keep us well enough in beef and potatoes, and a few holes in your jacket aren't going to kill you, so you can stop plucking at them for my benefit."

"Doesn't the mayoress want to be rid of the Ghoul of Vysehrad?" Nevine asked.

Xanthae gave her a shrug. "I don't pretend to understand the motives of that woman. You would be well advised to suspect that nothing she does is without purpose. And her purposes are seldom what they might seem. I can only wonder what devious plans she has for us."

"Oh," Nevine said, "that reminds me. She also invited us to a ball. She said she would hand you my guardianship papers while we are there." She plucked the perfumed letter from her coat and handed it to her.

Xanthae ripped open the seal and read the invitation quickly, before giving a disgusted sigh and handing it over to Petyr. He then handed it back to Nevine, who, of course, could not read it since she didn't understand Czech.

Xanthae was rubbing her forehead as if she had a headache.

"Couldn't this be fun?" Nevine asked innocently.

Xanthae looked sideways at her. "We'll go because we must. I don't know why she has chosen to invite us to this ball, but I can assure you it is not because she enjoys my conversation. You should know one thing; do you remember what I told you about magic?"

"It's bad," Nevine and Petyr said in unison.

"It's bad because magic is an attempt to violate nature's laws…God's laws. Only fools and men of evil intent would seek it out. The mayoress has several of the latter group about her and you can expect them to be there at this ball. The Society for Metaphysical Research, they are called. Old men and women nearing the end of their natural lives who look for some magical means of cheating death. They fancy themselves some sort of social group, on the cutting edge of science. I assure you there is nothing scientific about their research, which is of the most unholy sort imaginable."

"Sounds like this ball could be a lot of fun," Petyr said with a wink.

"Then maybe the mayoress wants us to meet this…Society for Metaphysical Research…but why would she want that?" Nevine asked.

"I don't know," Xanthae said, "and that's what makes me nervous. It could be a bit of a power thing for her. She knows how I feel about that group and their…research. This could simply be a chance for her to show me she has the power to make me do what she wants, since she controls your fate."

Nevine felt bad about the trouble she had caused Xanthae and told her so.

"No, no!" Xanthae said and reached out to hug her. "Never apologize! It's not your fault at all. You are not to be held accountable for the scheming of that woman."

Xanthae's words reassured Nevine. She hated to be the bearer of more bad news, but she felt duty-bound to point out the mayoress' necklace to Xanthae.

Xanthae took a close look at it and then asked Petyr for his thoughts.

"Looks like a real diamond," Petyr said with a whistle.

Xanthae shook her head. "I am not sure what to think about that. It is evident you have attracted the mayoress' attention."" We must consider the possibility that she knows more about your circumstances than we may like."

"How could she?" Nevine asked. "I didn't tell her anything."

"I know, dear. I can't explain it any more than I can explain your curious arrival. Keep the necklace for now. Not to wear it would only be to invite the mayoress' wrath unnecessarily. Just let us all be sure not to underestimate that woman. She is up to something, of that we can be sure."

The rest of the day was much more pleasant than the start. There was more instruction in the Czech language, and Xanthae taught Nevine some of the basics of the scientific method of inquiry, particularly the necessity of formulating and testing hypotheses. Meanwhile, Petyr began designing their flamethrower. Nighttime brought dinner of chicken and dumplings with potato, then an evening of pleasant conversation. The tension of the earlier part of the day was gone by the time Nevine settled in for bed. As she closed her eyes, she thought how good it felt to be some place that felt like home.

Chapter 6

Elliptical Orbits and Other Really Big Ovals

"All right, you two, it's time to wake up! You'll be late for class!"

The voice shook Nevine from her sleep. She sat up in her bed with a start. Her unbelieving eyes fell on Victoria Turnbell, who was folding up her blanket and preparing to return to her own room. Looking to her right, Nevine could see Aurora grumpily pulling the blanket tighter around her neck and face.

"Thanks, Victoria," Nevine had the presence of mind to say, although she was quite disoriented. Her brain attempted to search around for some kind of explanation for what might be going on, but the ultimate conclusion was unavoidable: she was back at Grimoire Manor and it was the morning after she had challenged the Hallway Ghost. It was difficult to believe, but...was everything that had happened in Prague just a dream? It had seemed too vivid...and too long, for that matter to just be a dream. Yet here she was, back at Grimoire Manor as if nothing happened. She took a quick stock of herself and discovered she was dressed back in her usual pajamas. The necklace that the mayoress had given her was gone, as were the magnesium burns from the flare that were on her hands. So that was it then...the first adult who had ever taken an interest in her was a figment of her imagination?

"Aurora!" Nevine ran over to her friend's bed and began shaking her awake.

"What…what is it?" Aurora said through puffy, barely open eyes, "This had better not mean that you're a morning person."

"You'll never guess what happened!" Nevine cried. As they went about getting dressed and ready for class and having breakfast, Nevine told Aurora about everything that had happened in Prague. Aurora listened with great interest, asking a few questions for clarification. Even in class, when they could whisper unobserved, Nevine kept telling her story. It took until lunchtime for her to finish. Finally, Aurora asked the question that was on both of their minds. "So, was it all a dream, or was it real?"

Nevine didn't know how to answer that. After thinking a bit, all she could say was, "It seemed real, but how could it be?"

"I dunno," Aurora said. "People keep telling me that ghosts aren't real, but I guess we know better than that."

Recess was much calmer than it was on Nevine's first day. Fiona and Jo-Beth, although clustered with a little group of admirers and shooting dark looks at Nevine and Aurora, kept to themselves. Although it had been stressful to end up in a fistfight on her first day, Nevine was feeling a bit more confident now, and she enjoyed a game of softball with Aurora, Clarisse and Polly and some of the other girls.

The only thing that marred the first part of her day was discovering that she had been given a nickname.

Returning inside from recess, a thin, wiry girl whom she didn't really know, had called out, "Hey, Cop-Girl," as Nevine had passed by with Aurora.

It hadn't been intended as a mean taunt, rather just a tease, but Nevine rounded on the girl all the same. "I'm a Copt, not a cop. Cop-T" she insisted, overemphasizing the T. The other girl shrunk back, apparently not sure what the big deal was, and Nevine walked away feeling frustrated.

"What does that even mean?" Aurora asked as they walked along the hall.

"I don't know," Nevine admitted with a tinge of sadness.

They were in math class with Ms. Emily after recess. She seemed a little cool toward Nevine, which was perhaps not surprising given Nevine's behavior the day before. The more she thought about it, the worse she felt. Fiona had been a first-class jerk, but maybe that hadn't given her the right to hit her. Although Aurora kept telling her that Fiona had earned a good whopping, she didn't like seeing how disappointed Ms. Emily seemed to be with her.

After math came science, the last class of the day. Despite her own interest in the topic, Nevine could see that science got the least enthusiasm out of the tired group of students. Outside, the sun was out and the yard of Grimoire Manor looked much more inviting than did introductory physics and the motion of the planets. Ms. Speer ruled science class with an iron fist. Her greetings the day before at the front door seemed positively fuzzy now that Nevine witnessed the disdain with which Ms. Speer regarded the pupils. This afternoon, the girls were particularly lackluster and Ms. Speer was driven to anger by their lack of enthusiasm.

"I've had quite enough of this!" Ms. Speer said at last. "Your participation is simply unsatisfactory! It seems as if none of you have done the reading for today."

The class got silent, none of them wanting to provoke her more than she already was. Nevine snapped out of her daydreams of Prague by Ms. Speer's tone. Ms. Speer stood next to Nevine's desk. "I see," Ms. Speer practically sneered, "that our new arrival hasn't added much brainpower to the class."

Nevine didn't think that was fair at all, but she kept quiet, figuring it was useless to protest. She felt her face turning scarlet, and she was practically able to feel Fiona Applegate's eyes boring into her.

"Fine, since none of you have anything to say, it will be detention for the whole class tonight after dinner." Her proclamation was met with soft groans by the class. "You can use the time to catch up on your reading." She let the full weight of her authority sink into the dismayed class for several moments before she added, "I will rescind this punishment, however, if even one of you can answer a simple question for me."

Another round of groans from the class. Aurora put her head on her desk, looking over at Nevine. "She always does this," Aurora whispered. "Her questions are impossible."

"Who," Ms. Speer began, the crisp sound of victory in her voice, "was the Danish astronomer whose observations of the orbit of Mars allowed his assistant Johannes Kepler to discover that planets orbit the sun in ellipses rather than circles?"

"What's an ellipse?" someone whispered in the

class.

"That would be an oval to you, Miss Roth, which you would know if you read the book."

Ms. Speer's question rang a bell for Nevine, however. Xanthae had mentioned something about this to her on the evening they went to the recital. One of the people who had been buried in the church (creepy as that was) Xanthae had told her a little about. He had been an astronomer and had done something with the elliptical orbit of planets. Nevine wasn't sure if he was Danish, but she remembered Xanthae said that he worked with someone named Kepler.

"Wait, wait..." Nevine said out loud, trying to think of the man's name. She was suddenly conscious that all eyes were on her, a dozen girls desperate to avoid detention. "I know this one..." she continued, although the name was on the tip of her tongue, "...he's the guy buried at Our Lady in Front of Tyn..." The girls all looked uncertain as she said this, but Ms. Speer got an interested and half-annoyed look on her face. Finally, it came to her. "Tito Brahe!" She was practically jumping in her seat with excitement as she thought of it. "His name is Tito Brahe!" She looked triumphantly at Ms. Speer. A dozen uncertain pairs of eyes also looked to Ms. Speer for her judgment.

Ms. Speer looked as if she had just bitten into a lime. Her face twisted into a frown for a moment before she at last said, "The man was not a member of the Jackson Five, Miss Turner. His name was Tycho Brahe. Nonetheless..." Her tone had a heavy note of reluctance, "...your answer is close enough to convince me that you've at least glanced at the textbook. I'll rescind detention for this evening," she declared to cheers from the other girls, and she had to shout to add, "but you had better read your texts; I won't allow Miss Turner to save you if you are all unprepared tomorrow."

Ms. Speer gave her no further compliment for knowing the answer, but the reactions of the other girls were reward enough. After being all but hoisted on their shoulders as they left the class, Nevine found herself feeling quite happy.

"That was just brilliant," Aurora told her warmly, after the other girls had finally dispersed. "How did you ever know that? Ms. Speer always picks stuff she knows we didn't read."

"His grave was in Prague," Nevine said thoughtfully. "Professor Halruaa told me about him."

"Hmm," Aurora said with great interest, thinking a bit, "maybe this dream of yours wasn't really just a dream?"

They brought their books back to their room and got ready for their meal. Dinner consisted of some kind of mashed meat on bread and too chewy baked potatoes. Nevine longed for Petyr's cooking. As was becoming routine, Nevine sat with Aurora, Polly, and Clarisse for dinner. As they were getting into their desserts of gelatin with suspended bits of fruit, Nevine asked, "So what are we going to do about the Hallway Ghost?"

"What do you mean?" Polly asked, her tone implying that Nevine might have asked what they were going to do about the tides or about the passage of time.

"Didn't Aurora tell you? We got attacked by the Hallway Ghost last night!"

"Yoooouuu got attacked by the Hallway Ghost," Aurora jested, playfully sticking out her tongue. "I had to save you."

"If you call trying to hide under your pillow, saving me," Nevine joked back. "Seriously, it was Victoria Turnbell that saved us."

"She's nice," Polly said, allowing herself to get a bit sidetracked. "I want to be like her when I'm a senior. I think she's supposed to go to Harvard or something."

"That's why no one leaves their room between eleven and one a.m.," Clarisse declared, scooping the inside of her bowl for every last bit of gelatin.

"That's what I tried to tell her last night." Aurora frowned.

"So the Hallway Ghost only comes around between eleven p.m. and one a.m.? Every night?" Nevine asked.

"Yep," Clarisse said, "every night. What does it matter?"

"I think," Nevine said, "that we should try to figure out as much as we can about the Hallway Ghost. The more we can figure out about it, the more ready we'll be."

"You want to fight it, don't you?" A note of admiration crept into Aurora's voice.

"I, for one, would like to be able to pee when I need to pee without being chased down the hall by some crabby old ghost." The other girls giggled with Nevine at her comment except for Polly, who nodded her head as if Nevine had just revealed the deepest of wisdoms. "Okay, so what do we know already? The ghost comes around the dorm area between eleven at night and one a.m. Where does it go after that?"

"I bet it lives in the west wing," Aurora suggested. "That's probably why they keep it all boarded up."

Nevine thought back to the previous night, which actually seemed like days ago to her. "But remember, Aurora...the ghost couldn't get through our door. It tried using the handle. If it could sneak out of the locked doors of the west wing, why couldn't it get through our door?"

"I thought ghosts could just walk through walls?" Clarisse said, curiously.

"Maybe some can," Aurora observed, "but Nevine's right. The Hallway Ghost couldn't get through our door."

"So it can't live in the west wing," Polly deduced for them all.

"That seems to be a reasonable hypothesis," Nevine observed.

"Big words. Hey, look who pays attention in science class." Clarisse laughed.

"Yeah, saved our butts today," Aurora said with a wink to Nevine.

"So it's got to live somewhere," Nevine reasoned, "unless ghosts just cease to exist during the day. But if it doesn't live in the west wing, then where?"

"The basement and attic are both locked too," Polly said, "but maybe it could come in from outside. A lot of windows are left unlocked and I think that the night security lady leaves the backdoor unlocked when she's patrolling the grounds."

"There's nothing in the recess area that a ghost could live in," Aurora reasoned, "unless she haunts a swing set by day."

"Maybe it's something on the grounds outside of the fence," Clarisse suggested, and the other three girls looked at her, considering the ramifications of what she had just said.

It was Aurora who broke the silence, saying out loud what was on all their minds, "The only way to know is to hop the fence and explore the grounds."

"You did notice that there's barbed wire on top of the fence, didn't you?" Polly pointed out, sounding exasperated.

"Maybe we can just throw you over the barbed wire and climb over you," Aurora snapped.

"Wait, wait," Nevine interrupted, not wanting them to get into the shouting match that seemed to be brewing, "we may have to figure out a way over the fence, but even if we find out where the ghost lives, then what? How do we get rid of it?"

The four of them thought quietly for a few moments. At last Aurora said, "I think we need to find out why the Hallway Ghost is haunting Grimoire Manor."

"Yes, I think Aurora's right," Nevine said, sounding excited.

"Come on, guys." Polly rolled her eyes. "Don't you watch the movies…well, I mean…didn't you watch them before you came here? All ghosts are the same. Somebody moves into a house no one has lived in for years and thinks it's a steal. The ghost always starts with light stuff, a few creaks and moans, and slowly builds up to the really scary stuff…."

"You know," Clarisse said, "I always wondered why the ghosts didn't just start right in with the really scary stuff if they were serious about getting people out of their house…"

"…the person who bought the house," Polly continued, ignoring Clarisse, "figures out they've got a ghost and that only they can help the ghost go to heaven or whatever. They find some old newspaper clippings and eventually figure out the ghost was some kid who got murdered by their parents or something. All we need to do is figure out which well the bones have been dumped down, dig them up and the problem will be solved."

"This ghost does the same thing every night," Nevine said, "and has been for years. I don't think it's building up to anything. Polly may be right about one thing, though. We may not be able to find any newspaper clippings, but maybe there are some other clues in the house?"

"We need to find out more about the family that used to own this house," Aurora said.

"We could try asking Ms. Emily," Polly suggested. "She might know something."

"She might," Aurora agreed, "although if we start asking a lot of questions, she might also guess that we are up to something, particularly if I'm the one asking the questions."

"We don't really know what to ask yet," Nevine pointed out. "I think the first thing that we need to do is try to figure out the identity of the ghost. Two ways I can think of to do that is to try to find if there is any information on the ghost stored in this house somewhere, and to have someone follow the ghost when it leaves the house."

"That could be dangerous," Polly exclaimed. "The ghost tried to attack you!"

"But it can't get through doors," Aurora reminded her. "You just have to always have a door you can retreat through."

"Besides, we don't really know that it meant to attack us," Nevine said.

"I don't think it was coming to tuck us in for the night." Aurora scowled.

Clarisse suggested, "We could track its movements on the landing for a few nights, figure out exactly what time it leaves. That way, we wouldn't have to try to hide out on the landing. We could just follow it, starting from our own rooms."

"Good idea, Clarisse," Nevine said. "We can plan to do it Saturday, which will give us a couple of days to figure out exactly what time we should start tracking it. Two of us can track the ghost while the other two try to find out where some information on the family that owned this house could be stored."

"The attic, I bet," Polly suggested. "The basement can flood sometimes so they wouldn't keep papers there, and the west wing is just too big. Even if something is in there, we wouldn't have the time to search the whole thing. My mom used to keep old important papers in our attic before she died."

"I can get the key, I think," Clarisse said. "If it's Saturday night, they'll let us stay up later. I can get friendly with the night staff lady, Ms. Elmwing. She likes to talk about sports. I should be able to swipe the key while she's relaxing and then pass it off to whoever's going for the attic."

"We'll need two flashlights too, if anyone has a chance to swipe them during the week," Nevine said. "We can always return them after our missions."

"So which of us is going to go to the attic, and who follows the ghost?" Polly asked.

"Nevine, you should search the attic, since you

might know what to look for better than the rest of us," Aurora suggested, although Polly and Clarisse didn't know that this likely had to do with Nevine's experience with Xanthae. "I'll come with you, if Polly and Clarisse are okay with tracking the ghost?" She looked over at the other two girls for their reaction.

Polly didn't look too sure, but Clarisse acted as if it was no big deal. "Sure," Clarisse said, rubbing her fingernails against her shirt. "It sounds like a good plan and we won't let you down." Polly looked at her hands nervously.

"All right!" Aurora said, tone tinged with excitement. "I think we've got a good plan. We should be able to come out of the night with some good information."

"Or we'll come out of it dead," Polly murmured grumpily.

****

After dinner, Nevine had one other matter to attend to. Excusing herself from her little cluster of friends, she pushed through the throng and approached Fiona Applegate, who was busy holding court over her own crowd. Fiona turned as Nevine approached and regarded her with a frown. Her various friends tittered and held their hands over their mouths while whispering and giggling to each other.

Nevine ignored them. Feeling a bit nervous, she swallowed her pride and looked Fiona in the eye. "Fiona, I didn't like what you said about me yesterday, but that didn't give me the right to hit you," she said, part of her sighing inwardly. "I just wanted to say that I'm sorry."

Fiona's little crew were hushed, waiting for their

leader's reply. Fiona looked surprised for a minute, regarding Nevine as if she were some kind of space alien. "I see," she said at last, her voice chilly. "So you think apologizing to me is getting you out of a beating?"

"No, that's not it at all—" Nevine protested, but it was useless.

Fiona cut her off. "You're going to get yours." Her eyes narrowed angrily. "You won't know when or how, but you are going to get what's coming to you, Cop-Girl." Fiona stomped off with a self-righteous strut, her gaggle of admirers flocking after her, giggling and whispering to each other.

Nevine sighed, her stomach sinking. "Well, I know I feel better…"

Chapter 7

Moving Pictures

Nevine was glad to let Aurora take the lead in planning their move on the Hallway Ghost. Aurora's commanding presence gave Nevine a sense of security that felt good. As the week wore on, the dark-haired girl began to seem less like an orphan named Aurora and more like a little general, giving orders to her troops. She showed them how to synchronize their alarm clocks, which wasn't easy to do with the cheap and erratic clocks they'd been given for their rooms. She insisted they stay up late each night listening to the Hallway Ghost, waiting to see when the footsteps faded, knowing it would be safe then to begin tracking the ghost.

After several measurements, they all agreed that the Hallway Ghost finished its final round of the landing at a quarter past one o'clock. It ought to be safe for Clarisse and Polly to emerge from their room and try to track the ghost's progress from there. It wasn't going to be easy tracking something invisible, but so long as the footsteps kept creaking against the floorboards, it should be possible. Two flashlights were "procured" as well, which were going to be necessary, particularly for Nevine and Aurora's trip to the attic. As Saturday approached, Nevine became more and more excited about their plans.

In spite of the excitement, Nevine was feeling worn down from classes. Ms. Speer appeared to feel it necessary to take vengeance on Nevine's fortunate guess of Tycho Brahe, which had snatched the class from detention one afternoon. Ms. Speer's expectations of the class became quite unreasonable, even cruel, and Nevine felt guilty that she was no longer able to save them from Ms. Speer's obscure questions. The class spent two evenings in detention, going over extra physics questions. By Friday, Ms. Speer appeared to have satisfied herself that she had tortured the girls enough and her questions became possible to answer at least, and Friday evening they got to enjoy some outside time.

Nevine was glad to see Saturday come and spent it in relaxation, extracurricular activities and the excitement of anticipation. Ms. Emily organized some games in the yard during the afternoon, but even Clarisse's heart seemed like it wasn't in the sports. The girls poked fussily at their dinners that evening and excused themselves to Nevine and Aurora's room to finalize their plans.

With adrenaline surging through her, Nevine had no difficulty staying up late. The girls all pretended to go about their bedtime routines, but in truth, they stayed dressed in regular clothes. Nevine and Aurora waited in their room, chattering anxiously and pacing about the room waiting. Aurora flicked their flashlight on and off so many times that Nevine wondered if it would still work when they needed it. Sometime just before eleven o'clock, Clarisse knocked softly on their door and passed them the attic key, which she had nicked from

Ms. Elmwing.

At last, at eleven p.m., they heard the telltale footsteps on the landing. They quieted down, sitting together on Aurora's bed, listening. The night after the ghost had tried to get into their room, they had been terrified, wondering if the ghost would try to get in their room again, but it hadn't. It seemed to have forgotten Nevine's attempt to prove it a live human. The footsteps walked the landing in a slow circle, then faded away, perhaps going down the stairs or to some other part of the mansion. The ghost must have walked a considerable path along the house, as the footsteps only came back two more times during those two hours. This was the same pattern as every night.

The third appearance of the ghost on the landing faded away a quarter after one a.m., just as expected. Nevine and Aurora knew that Clarisse and Polly would now be getting to work, sneaking out of their room and attempting to follow the ghost's path from a distance. Nevine and Aurora wanted to avoid inadvertently stumbling along the ghost's path, so they waited fifteen more minutes before setting out.

They had both thought to dress in dark clothes— Nevine in navy blue and Aurora in black sweaters and jeans. Naturally, they kept the flashlight off for the moment, as they didn't want to draw attention to themselves. The interior of the house was very dark, and it was difficult, particularly in the dorm landing, which had no skylight, to see exactly where they were going. Only the red glow of a distant emergency exit light helped guide them along. They stayed on the third floor, hoping this would keep them away from the ghost's path. Nevine concentrated hard not to make a sound as they slipped through the winding halls to the administrative wing, with the plush landing, chandelier, and the big skylight, which let in enough light from the moon for them to move about easier now.

On the big landing, they stopped for a moment and listened. They couldn't hear anything of the Hallway Ghost or Clarisse and Polly. Indeed, the mansion seemed mostly quiet. Down below, somewhere on the first floor, a little light seemed to be glowing, and this was probably for the night staff lady, Ms. Elmwing. Quietly tip-toeing, they moved to the main stair and ascended to the fourth floor. Without even needing to discuss it in advance, they avoided going near to the Provost's office. Although they didn't know whether the Provost lived on the school grounds like many of the teachers did, they were in no mood to take the chance and the unmarked office somehow radiated danger.

They moved past the ballroom instead, and up to the little locked door that led to the attic. Here they held their breaths as they tried out the key the Clarisse had "borrowed", fearing perhaps that she might have gotten the wrong one. They grinned at each other as the lock clicked and the door popped open for them. Their plan seemed actually to be working! They hadn't heard Clarisse or Polly screaming in terror, so all seemed to be going well.

The house's beautiful adornments ended at the stairwell that led up into the attic. This was clearly a part of the house that was utilitarian only. The stairway was dark and narrow, built of simple boards of wood hammered together with no embellishments. It looked almost as if it had been carved out of some kind of wooden cave. Aurora flicked on the flashlight and cast the beam about, looking for a light switch, but there was none.

Aurora led the way, her feet seeming to find every loose board on the way up. In truth, the entire staircase did not seem terribly well built and shook a little as they climbed it. It made a turn to the right halfway up and then ended in a simple plywood door with an ancient-looking knob. There was no lock on the top door, and it groaned open at Aurora's touch.

They were dismayed to find that the attic was massive. They had been imagining some small simple room filled with boxes of useful information, but as Aurora cast the beam around, they guessed the attic ran the length of the entire mansion. There actually seemed to be various kinds of rooms built into the attic, areas that were walled off and had their own doors. Fortunately, the attic had some windows on one side, providing some natural lighting from the moon, which helped them to see reasonably well even without the flashlight, which was overwhelmed by such a vast space.

There was stuff everywhere, and it wasn't well organized. There were piles of boxes far and wide, some of which had labels and some did not. Racks of old clothes stood here and there, and old children's toys and dolls were carelessly strewn about. Countless shelves held books of all sorts, from bibles to novels to books they guessed had to do with the family business. Dust and cobwebs were everywhere, and Nevine got the impression this was the most unloved part of the house. Probably when the state had taken over the house, anything left of the Grimoires that couldn't be sold was stuck up here, and there was a lot of it. Maybe it had some kind of historical value, but if it did, it had long since been forgotten.

"There's no way we're going to be able to search through all of this!" Aurora said, sounding dismayed.

"No, probably not," Nevine admitted, her own heart sinking. This had seemed like such a good plan, but they hadn't counted on the possibility of the information they needed being buried under mounds of useless stuff. "Still, this is better than having no shot at all. Let's see if we can find anything."

They agreed to search for anything that would give them some idea of who the Grimoires were, names, photographs, anything. As they began their initial examination around the attic, they realized their search was narrowed down for them somewhat. None of the little rooms built off the main attic would open, even with the key Clarisse had gotten. The doors were flimsy and Aurora looked half tempted to try to break one of them down, but Nevine talked her out of it.

"They probably keep all the valuable stuff in these locked rooms!" Aurora protested.

"Probably," Nevine agreed, "but we don't need their valuables, just something that tells us about them and which one might be the Hallway Ghost."

A few minutes later, Aurora was examining one of the books they had seen with the flashlight. "Hey," she whispered loud enough to get Nevine's attention, "can you read anything other than English?"

"A little Spanish maybe," Nevine replied. "Why?"

"A lot of these books aren't in English."

Nevine came over to take a look. The pages of the book Aurora was holding were old and faded, the typeset in some kind of hard to read style that modern books didn't use anymore. Still, Nevine could tell it wasn't English. "It looks like French, I think," she said, feeling further disheartened. Even if they found something valuable, they might not be able to use it if they couldn't read it.

"This one's a Bible." Aurora said, referring to an old book so large it required her to use both hands to lift. "I think it's got some kind of record of births and deaths in it. Back when my parents were alive, my mom had a Bible like this that had been passed down through the family. It listed all the births and deaths like from my great-great-great-great-great-great-grandmother all the way down through me. You know, I have no idea what happened to that bible."

"This could be useful." Nevine tried to sound optimistic. "Except the handwriting's hard to read, and it's still in French. I don't know which ones are births and which ones are deaths…and all the names look like smudges."

Aurora set the bible aside with a shrug. It was as Nevine had feared; even stuff that had information was going to be of limited value since they couldn't read it.

Nevine opened a third book, hoping for something better, and her heart gave a little leap. "Hey, Aurora, look at this!" she said, scrunching her lips up in thought. Aurora came over and looked at the book, then looked at Nevine, a little baffled as to what the big deal was.

"That's not in English either," Aurora pointed out.

"No," Nevine agreed, "but it's not in French. See all these squiggles over the letters? I've seen that before. I think this book is written in Czech. That's what people speak in Prague." The book was at least as old as the French Bible, and had numerous notes penned in the margin in messy, largely smudged handwriting. The notes seemed to go back and forth between French and Czech.

"Can you read it?"

"No, and I don't know that the book itself is important, but don't you see? I don't think a lot of people speak Czech. If they've got this book, the Grimoires must have been to Prague." She honestly wasn't sure what it meant, but she didn't think it could have been a coincidence. She felt this was an important discovery, even if she couldn't puzzle out what it meant exactly.

"So you think there might be some connection between you going to Prague and Grimoire Manor?" Aurora asked, and there was a tinge of confused excitement in her voice as well.

"I don't know," Nevine admitted, "but it seems like an odd coincidence. I just wish I could read it!"

Alas, her studies of the Czech language were not nearly far enough along to prove of much value in deciphering the tome, and in the end, like the French Bible, they reluctantly decided to cast it aside and continue their search. The only books they found in English were clearly popular books the family must have bought in the United States: Twain, Lovecraft, Hemmingway.

They gave up on the books for a bit, sifting through the attic for other things of interest. Once again Aurora proved herself to be the observant one, forgetting to whisper this time as she called Nevine over to her. What she had found was an old photograph, perhaps five inches by seven. They agreed it was really old, because the colors were different shades of brown, ranging from nearly black through light tan. What looked like a big crack ran through the center of the photograph itself, although the frame and glass that held the picture were intact. There were seven people in the photograph, clustered in a little group and looking at the camera. There were three women and four men, and none of them were smiling. They were dressed in very old-style clothes, although not so different from the clothes Nevine saw on some people in Prague.

Under the people, someone had scribbled in names: Pierre, Genevieve, Thierry, Eloise, Lyrre, Louis and Margot. Most of the people looked to be in their teens and twenties, although one man and woman were older looking and might have been parents. The picture had been taken outside in a lightly wooded area like a park.

"Why doesn't anyone smile in old pictures? Did they all have bad teeth?" Aurora wondered aloud.

"I think," Nevine said. "I heard it was because the cameras didn't work very well. The people would have to hold a pose longer than we do for pictures today, and it was hard to hold a smile. I don't really know, though. Maybe you're right, maybe they had bad teeth. Look at this though..." Nevine pointed to a cathedral in the background of the picture. "I think that's the Cathedral of Saints Paul and Peter at Vysehrad. And look here, that's the graveyard that surrounds it."

"Charming place for a family picture," Aurora observed.

"This means that the family really was in Prague, that there must have been some kind of connection!"

"We should hang onto this one, since it has the

family names," Aurora said, slipping the picture out of its frame and stuffing it under her shirt.

There were other photographs as well. The women in the family particularly had many individual portraits taken of themselves. There were later pictures as well, some of which must have been taken after they had come to America. Some of the same people were in the photos, but some seemed to vanish, perhaps dead or moved. All of the men were gone from the pictures taken later, replaced by other men who might have been husbands for the young women, and then children. Subsequent pictures detailed the children growing to adults themselves through several generations.

"Here's the last one," Aurora said, flashing a final portrait with her flashlight. "It says it was taken in 1972. Take a look at the clothes they're wearing. How did anyone ever think these were a good idea?"

Nevine was troubled by the photo, though. "Look, there's still at least one young couple in the photo and they have a little boy."

"So?"

"I thought this house went to the state because everybody died. I wonder why those people would have died so young."

Their thoughts were cut off by a sudden loud banging sound that reverberated through the attic. It was like the banging that had rung through the building on Nevine's first day, one loud clang followed seconds later by another. It was louder than that first day though, as if the point of origin for the banging was closer at hand, perhaps within the attic walls themselves. Nevine and Aurora jumped into each other's arms. Aurora looked as terrified as Nevine felt.

The banging stopped after six times, but they then noticed that the attic had gotten very, very cold, much more so than it had already been. Their breath formed misty clouds, and the air felt like it had when Nevine had confronted the Hallway Ghost, as if the air was draining the life out of her. It was worse now, however, and Nevine had the feeling once again of rage or hatred, like the house itself wanted to harm her. What was worse, their flashlight flickered and died, and they now had only the moonlight through the windows to light the attic.

They huddled together, keeping silent and not knowing what to do. A moment after the banging had stopped, they heard a soft creaking noise. Although they no longer had the flashlight working, by the light of the moon, they could see the doorway to the stairs slowly opening.

"We're trapped!" Aurora whispered.

As she said it, there was another creak from a floorboard moving, and a tower of boxes moved just a bit as if something or someone had jostled them. Nevine was convinced that something unseen had joined them in the attic and was moving toward them.

Nevine pulled herself out of Aurora's arms. Although her hands were shaking, she looked around and found a baseball bat. She picked up and lifted it over her shoulder. "Whatever it is, I'll distract it. You make a break for it!"

"I'm not leaving you up here by yourself," Aurora protested, sounding offended. Keeping the old picture of the people in Prague they had found under one arm, she lifted the flashlight over her head with the other. "If we are going to die, then we're going to die together!"

"Show yourself!" Nevine's somewhat brave voice rang out. "We're ready for you, you stupid coward!" As she shouted, her breath came out in puffy clouds of mist, which suspiciously moved around some invisible obstacle. For a moment, the mist seemed to form into something that looked like the outline of a jaw, leering at them threateningly.

Simultaneously, Nevine and Aurora screamed and began swinging. Unfortunately, it was far from a coordinated attack. Nevine foolishly closed her eyes as she swung and felt a moment's exhilaration as her baseball bat connected against something soft and solid. This proved to be a tower of boxes, however, and they immediately came tumbling down on her, trapping her under them. Something gripped her ankle and bit into it and she shrieked in pain. "Aurora, something's got my ankle!"

"I'll save you!" Aurora shouted, and dove for Nevine's feet. A second later, the flashlight came down on the hard bone on the side of Nevine's ankle.

Nevine screamed out again, "That's my ankle, you idiot!"

"Well, it's not like I can see anything," Aurora said, and before she struck again, there was a light in the attic, another flashlight, focused squarely on their little ruckus.

"What's going on here?" demanded the familiar voice of Ms. Emily.

"Ms. Emily," Nevine called, feeling momentary relief, "Something's got my ankle!"

"You've landed on an umbrella, you naughty girl." Ms. Emily helped Aurora move the fallen boxes off of her. Once done, Nevine stood and indeed saw that she had been outfought by an old umbrella, and felt considerable embarrassment and shame. There was no sign of the ghost they had confronted.

Nevine and Aurora stood silent as Ms. Emily gave them quite a talking-to. "You had better explain yourselves!"

The two girls looked at each other, not sure how much was safe to reveal. Nevine wasn't sure what was the right thing to do, but they finally told Ms. Emily about the Hallway Ghost and how they had wanted to investigate who the ghost was. They left out the information about Polly and Clarisse as well as the picture Aurora kept hidden under her shirt, and didn't mention Nevine's nighttime trip to Prague.

Ms. Emily sighed. "Oh, you two," she said, and her emotion was unreadable, although her anger seemed to have ebbed a bit. "First, hand over the key that you filched." Sheepishly, Aurora handed her the stolen key, "And now you two will come with me." She turned, intent on leading them back down the stairs for their punishment.

Moments later, Ms. Emily led them through the teachers' quarters to her own apartment. "Wait here," she instructed them, while she went into her rooms to get the instruments of their punishment.

Nevine and Aurora looked at each other and waited for a moment before taking note of how dark and terrifying the hallway was, and decided to scamper just inside Ms. Emily's doorway. The room within was lit up with a little end table lamp and looked like an average apartment, except that it had no television. There was a computer set up, however, and chairs and a little couch and a small dining room set with four chairs. On one wall was a picture of a younger Ms. Emily in a wedding dress, arm in arm with a man they had never seen before. Aurora pointed out the picture, and they both gawked at it for a moment, quite surprised.

There was a little hallway and several rooms off of it. From one of these rooms, there came a little moaning sound, and Nevine grabbed Aurora's hand instinctively. Then they could hear Ms. Emily's voice saying to someone, "It's okay, it was just a little noise. I'll be right back…"

Curiosity got the better of them, and despite the trouble they were already in, they crept further into the apartment, tip-toeing down the hall toward the voices. They rounded the corner to a little bedroom and found Ms. Emily there with a boy of about twelve, who was sitting on the floor and rocking in Ms. Emily's arms. Ms. Emily was patting the boy's hair and trying to soothe him. The boy only moaned, rocking back and forth, and seemed almost not to notice that Ms. Emily was there. One hand nervously went up to his left temple and twisted at the hair there, and the girls could see that he must have habitually done this, for there was a bald spot.

Physically, the boy looked healthy, and Nevine figured he would even have been an attractive fellow. His behavior was odd, however, even a bit frightening, and Nevine wondered if the poor boy was a victim of the ghosts.

Ms. Emily looked up as they appeared in the doorway. "Girls," she said, "this is my son, Joshua. He was frightened by the banging."

Nevine and Aurora were too shocked to speak for a

moment. They had no idea that Ms. Emily had a son, or even that a boy lived in the mansion. Finally, it was Aurora who spoke up, very timidly, "Is he okay, Ms. Emily? Did the ghosts do something to him?"

She looked up at Aurora and gave her a smile that was both kind and somehow sad. "No, nothing like that, Miss Ziniti…Aurora." She patted the boy on the head one more time and stood up. He barely noticed she moved away from him, other than his hand went back up to his temple. "Have you ever had a really boring class, and the only thing that you can do is daydream? You end up daydreaming until it's almost like the world around you…the classroom, is gone?"

Both girls nodded.

"Well, life for Joshua is like that. He's got his own internal world that he daydreams about all the time. It's more interesting to him than the real world. The only problem is that he can't really stop daydreaming." She gently guided the girls away from the doorway and closed the door behind her. "He goes to a special school in the city during the day, which is why you've never seen him before."

"I'm sorry if we woke up your son," Nevine said, meaning it. "We honestly didn't make the big banging noises…well, until the boxes fell on me."

Ms. Emily led them back to the living room and they sat on the couch for a moment. "It's okay, girls. I know you didn't mean anything. And I know the bangs weren't you. This house makes lots of noises."

"Something attacked us in the attic," Aurora said, very seriously.

Ms. Emily exhaled a heavy sigh. "The attic is a very scary place and it can be dangerous, and not because of ghosts. There are reasons…real important reasons…that we keep some areas of the house locked up."

"Then you don't believe in the ghosts?" Nevine asked.

Ms. Emily looked at them very seriously. "This house is very old, and it has many secrets. I'll grant you that much. But you're more likely to electrocute yourself or fall through a bad patch in the floor than get harmed by any ghost, I'll tell you that. That's why some areas of the house are off limits." She looked at the faces of the two frightened girls and sighed again. "Did you know that I used to live here when I was a little girl?"

The truth of it was that Nevine had great difficulty imagining Ms. Emily as a little girl, let alone wondering about where she might have lived. At last Nevine recovered enough from the shock to ask, "Do you mean that you were an orphan too?"

"Yes," Ms. Emily said, "in fact, just like you, Nevine, I never knew my parents. I was well acquainted with the Hallway Ghost when I lived here, and all the other strange things that this house did. I'm not going to tell you if they're real or just your imagination, but I will say this. Being here in this house offers an opportunity. Grimoire Manor is recognized for its educational work with young girls. If you graduate from here, a whole new world will open up for you and you can leave whatever ghosts you have behind you. I hope that you'll stay focused on what is really important while you are here and not get distracted by too many adventures."

"Why did you come back here?" Nevine asked

quietly.

Ms. Emily smiled sadly. "When I graduated here, I got my degree in education, and then I married a wonderful man. He was in the Army and he died soon after our son was born. The Provost gave me a job, and let Joshua stay here as well. I guess that, in a way, I've become an orphan again." She stood and led them back out of her apartment.

They were not surprised that she led them to one of the little classrooms and they found themselves with *War and Peace* in front of them. "You'll be glad to know ""that I saved your old notebooks so that you'll be able to pick up from where you left off. Since you seem to be having trouble sleeping, I thought thirty more pages of Tolstoy might entice you to more regular sleep-wake patterns. Good night, girls."

"Good night, Ms. Emily," they said in unison, both of them feeling too sad somehow to be angry at her for their punishment. It was dawn before they were done and at last, they walked off to bed. They were too tired even to discover how Clarisse and Polly's mission had gone...that was going to have to wait until their poor minds could rest for a bit. And thus it was after lunch before they learned where the Hallway Ghost slept.

Chapter 8

Dinner With Victoria

Still tired, and feeling a bit cranky, Nevine woke very late with an aching wrist and almost missed lunch. As it was Sunday, the girls were allowed to engage in sports or socialize on the grounds. It was an overcast, crisp day, but not so bad that it could keep the girls inside. Clarisse and Polly were waiting anxiously for Nevine and Aurora, and greeted them with great excitement.

"What happened to you two?" Polly asked, her eyes wide. Nevine could tell that whatever had occurred the night before had given her much more enthusiasm than she had shown before.

With her eyelids still half closed, Aurora said, "Let's just say Nevine and I are becoming more acquainted with the continuing saga of Pierre Bezukhov and Natalya Rostova than we care to."

"Who?" Clarisse asked, confused.

"Never mind," Nevine said. "Our night wasn't a total loss." She filled them in on all that had occurred in the attic and the picture they had found. She told them that the family must have come from Prague, although kept details from Clarisse and Polly as to how she knew this. She was lucky that Aurora had proven open-minded to her story, and didn't want to let it get out any further. If Fiona Applegate found out about it…

Clarisse and Polly listened with great interest, and they puzzled over the Grimoire family history for some moments before Clarisse told them, "We found out where the Hallway Ghost goes!"

Nevine and Aurora listened with rapt attention as the two other girls detailed their adventures. As had been suspected, an invisible ghost had been difficult to track by sound alone. It was only because the house had so many creaky floorboards that it had been possible. So long as Clarisse and Polly kept their distance and stayed in the shadows, the Hallway Ghost either didn't notice them or didn't care. While Ms. Elmwood was elsewhere on her nightly rounds, the Hallway Ghost had simply slipped out the back door and into the very yard in which they were now standing.

Once in the yard, the girls looked for any disturbances in the grass where the ghost may have stepped on, but the grass had been frosted by the night's cold and this had proven to be reasonably easy. The footsteps had ultimately led them to the chain-link fence.

"The fence has a hole in it!" Aurora guessed so loud that she soon found three sets of hands covering her mouth.

Without attracting undo attention, Clarisse and Polly led the other two behind one of the tall shrubs and pointed out where the chain-link fence appeared to have been torn away from the supporting metal pole. The hole was only about two feet tall, but plenty big for a person, or ghost perhaps, to crawl through. The tall bush hid it very well, and when rested against the support pole, it was hard to notice that the fence was damaged.

"Just along the cliff face there's a trail into the woods," Polly told them with great excitement, "and a bit in there's an old graveyard. That's where the ghost went."

"Well, I guess that makes sense somehow." Aurora nodded thoughtfully.

"Did you see which grave it went to?" Nevine asked hopefully. It would be great to get a name for the ghost.

"Are you kidding?" Clarisse said. "Once the Hallway Ghost got to the graveyard, we lost it and we weren't about to go stomping up there disturbing dozens of ghosts for all we knew. We figured that would be a job for our fearless leader…"

"Nevine Turner!" Her name was shouted across the yard from the open back door. It was Ms. Speer, and her expression didn't look warm.

"This can't be good." Nevine sighed, and the other three girls nodded their heads in agreement.

Nevine crossed the yard, aware of the many eyes on her as she went. Not least, she was aware of Fiona Applegate watching and snickering at what was surely Nevine's misfortune. Nevine presented herself sheepishly to Ms. Speer, who said only, "The Provost wishes to have a word with you. I assume that you can find your own way?"

That wasn't what Nevine was expecting, but she nodded and began her lonely trek up the main stairs. Had the Provost gotten word of her adventure the night before and wanted to punish her further? Was the Provost going to kick her out of Grimoire Manor, and if so, where would she go then? As she trudged up the stairs, it occurred to her to wonder why Aurora wasn't being called in for a similar reprimand, although perhaps that was only because Aurora was going to be next.

At last, Nevine came to the unmarked office door that Ms. Emily had pointed out on her first day and, feeling a mixture of fear and curiosity, she knocked.

"Come in," called a voice from beyond the door.

Nevine opened the door and walked into a spacious office that was perhaps the room that most reminded Nevine of how a mansion's rooms should look. There was an enormous bay window that looked out over the front lawn. Shelves of academic books lined the walls, so many books it was hard to believe any one person could or would even want to read all of them. On the walls were paintings, a large map of the world, and another map of the solar system. A large mahogany desk occupied the center of the room. The desk was empty except for a daily planner and two curious nutcracker figurines with white hair and beards and little white jackets. The Provost was an elderly woman, exactly how old Nevine could only guess at somewhere around a thousand, with long gray hair and outfitted in a gray dress.

The old woman regarded her coldly as she entered the room and beckoned her to take a seat in a hard wooden chair. "Well, Nevine Turner," the Provost said, "I understand you had a long night yesterday."

"Ms. Emily told you?" Nevine asked instinctively, and heard a note of accusation and disappointment in her own tone.

"Not at all," the Provost said, unsmiling. "In fact, you just informed me that Ms. Emily has failed to report a serious disciplinary matter she was aware of to me."

Nevine could not help but let her face fall into her outstretched palm.

"Let me be quite honest with you, Miss Turner," the Provost said coolly. She had stood and paced a bit before the bay window. "On a personal level, if you see fit to invent ways to get yourself killed, I really have few qualms about that. However, if you managed to do it on my time, in Grimoire Manor, there will be a state investigation and that will put the future of all the girls who live here in serious jeopardy. Do you want that, Miss Turner? To cast these girls back into the foster care system?"

It felt as if the temperature in the room had dropped twenty degrees. Shivering, Nevine clutched her goosebump-covered arms and shook her head.

"Let us admit to each other here and now," the Provost said, "that your life is entirely valueless. Were I to decide to expel you from Grimoire Manor, you would be left to the whims of a very cruel world to wither and rot like so many other wasted children. Do you understand me?" The Provost stopped and glowered over her.

"Yes, I think I do," Nevine said, trying to dissolve into the chair somehow.

The Provost shook her head. "Perhaps I should have taken it upon myself to have a little chat with you earlier. I have a file on you here. Shall I tell you what it says?" Indeed, the old woman was tapping a manila file against her desk. Where it had come from, Nevine wasn't sure—it hadn't been there a moment ago, and the Provost had opened no drawers.

Nevine nodded, not sure what else to do.

The Provost set it down and flipped it open, although it was clear that she had memorized it and didn't need to refer to what was in it. "You don't bond well with your foster parents. You have the wisdom of an underfed hamster and are at risk for chronic depression, and…" —the Provost drew the last word out for an extra second— "…an intellect that is very superior."

Nevine remembered the testing, the day spent with an unfriendly man in a rumpled shirt and a stained tie, but she had never been told the results before. She didn't know what to think about them now.

"Don't get arrogant," the Provost continued. "Every girl here has remarkable intelligence, yes, even Miss Applegate, with whom you have bonded in your usual manner. That's why you have all been chosen to stay at Grimoire Manor. We scour society's throwaway children for those who are worth saving and offer you this chance. If you graduate from Grimoire Manor, the state of Rhode Island will pay for four years of undergraduate education within the state university system. I suspect that if you do well and keep your grades satisfactory, you will find yourself with scholarship offers from top universities as well. We have an excellent record of placements at Harvard, Yale, Columbia—some girls have gone to Oxford and Cambridge…" These pronouncements were made as sheer fact, with no hint of pride in the Provost's voice. "Our graduates are doctors, researchers, Senators, Congresswomen…our expels and drop-outs are failures, every one. Does that make clear for you the roads that are now open to you?"

"Yes, ma'am," Nevine said meekly.

"There will be no more trips to the attic," the Provost pronounced. "There is nothing for you there. Are we in agreement?"

"Yes, ma'am."

The Provost sighed and sat back down in her chair. "I'm getting too old to be whipping you ingrates into shape. I'm getting too soft with age."

Of course, this comment made Nevine wonder what kind of death machine she had been when she was young, but Nevine, fortunately, having more wisdom than an underfed hamster, no matter what the report said, she bit her tongue.

"Go on," —the Provost gave her a dismissive wave— "Let's try to avoid having many conversations like this one, shall we? Now get out."

Nevine nodded and stood, almost running for the door before the Provost changed her mind. She opened the door quickly and closed it behind her. Once in the safety of the hall, she let out a long, deep breath. Only then did Nevine realize the Provost had never once raised her voice, and had barely shown any emotion at all. She had never needed to.

****

That evening, away from the Provost and the teachers, Nevine could finally relax, if one could call studying physics and mathematics relaxing. The monotony of all of this was broken up after six o'clock when Victoria Turnbell knocked on their door.

"Hello," she said, dressed in jeans and a jacket. "Don't you remember that we'll be spending Sunday evenings together?" This, of course, was a welcome change from studying. Following Victoria's lead, the girls wore their coats.

Victoria had something of an unexpected treat for them; she had gotten permission to walk them just up the street to a little hamburger restaurant. There was a little trail down the hill that led to the rocky seashore, then back up a bit to where the restaurant stood in the distance. It was a cold walk along the seashore, with wind whipping in off the cold ocean, and the girls drew their coats in tight. They were alone along the beach, except for the seagulls, and heaps of brown seaweed pushed in by the tides. Behind them, Grimoire Manor perched up over its cliffs, and in front, the lights of the little restaurant shone along the shore.

By the time they got to it, Nevine was glad for the restaurant's warmth. They settled into a booth and were given menus, although, in truth, the restaurant offered few choices. Moments later, they had all ordered burgers and soda, food that all of their mothers would have disapproved of, had any of their mothers still been alive.

"I'm to instruct you," Victoria told them, "that you are not to interpret this outing in any way as a reward for the mischief you have committed over the past few days. Ms. Emily believes some time with a senior student will be helpful for you two and I was able to convince her to allow me to take you here, but you're on thin ice, to be sure."

"I didn't even know that we could leave Grimoire Manor," Aurora said wondrously.

"It won't happen often," Victoria admitted, "but as you advance in years, you'll get a few more privileges, provided that you are well-behaved. The truth is, though, since the teachers don't allow for movies, malls, or socializing with boys, the options are rather limited, anyway. Still, once you get to your junior year, you can find a job in the city during certain hours. I work at Newport Hospital a few times a week, which is how I can pay for your dinners."

"Wow," Nevine said, "thanks for paying for us. It must be nice to have some money."

Victoria shrugged. "Well, there's not much we can spend it on, so most of it we save for later. Once we hit college, we can buy whatever we want. We'll be free of Grimoire Manor. Just one more year for me. You two still have a long way to go, but keep your head down; it will happen."

"Does it ever get any better?" Aurora asked with a scowl.

"No," Victoria said very plainly, "it doesn't. I wish I had gotten a normal life like most kids, but I didn't and there's not much I can do about that. I can do my best to be sure that the rest of my life is good, though. If that means sticking it out at Grimoire Manor for one more year, well, I guess I can do that. Actually, this year is kind of exciting; I'm looking at different colleges, wondering where I may ultimately end up. I feel kind of like I'm nearing the get out of jail term."

"Is it true the girls who drop out or are expelled end up dead or worse?" Nevine relayed the story about her meeting with the Provost.

Nevine expected Victoria to laugh and dismiss the idea. "I don't know," was what she said instead, with a serious look. "Some girls do run away from Grimoire Manor; I guess that's normal for an orphanage. Most don't, though. As you well know, we've got no place to go, really. Those that do run away are never allowed back. Despite what the Provost said to you, it's not very common for one of the girls to get expelled. You have to really be a discipline problem for that to happen. If Fiona Applegate is safe, then I don't think your little adventures will be enough to get you expelled. You'll do a heap of detention if you keep it up, though."

"They should put us to work, copying books." Aurora sighed.

"What about the girl who used to have my bed? What happened to her?" Nevine asked.

There was an uncomfortable pause as Aurora and Victoria looked at each other for a moment, almost as if they were challenging each other. At that second, three hot and juicy burgers arrived, distracting them. The smell was heavenly, far tastier food than they ever got at Grimoire Manor.

Nevine poured some ketchup on her burger and began eating, but the other two seemed to be in some kind of game of chicken, waiting for the other to speak.

At last, Victoria answered, saying, "She ran away…"

As she spoke, Aurora talked over her, saying, "She was kidnapped!"

Victoria sighed. "Some of the girls naturally thought she was stolen by the ghosts or something, but the police came and said she had just run away."

Aurora was more insistent, her voice animated as she pointed out, "She didn't take any of her stuff with her, and I was in the bed right next to her and didn't hear a thing. I would have heard her leave if she ran away."

"Aurora," Victoria said, "I've seen you in the morning. You wouldn't wake up if a giant centipede started tap-dancing at the foot of your bed."

"But she did leave all of her stuff behind," Aurora insisted, quietly conceding the other point. Aurora's eyes widened. "I was in the bed next to her...it could have been me!"

Nevine watched the exchange with a raised eyebrow, although she wasn't sure what to make of it. She trusted Aurora and Victoria both and wasn't sure which of their interpretations made more sense. If it was a ghost kidnapping, Nevine took some comfort in observing that it at least seemed pretty rare. Victoria and Aurora argued it out for a bit more, but Victoria got tired of Aurora's insistence on the ghost kidnapping version of events and eventually waved her off.

"What do you think you're going to do when you leave Grimoire Manor?" Nevine asked then, trying to change the topic.

Victoria looked thoughtful for a moment. "Well, the first thing I want to do is just get into a good college. After that, I don't know for sure. I think though, if I could be anything, I'd like to become a Supreme Court judge. I guess that means law school. What about you two? Have you given any thought to it."

"No," Aurora said.

"I don't know either," Nevine said. "I don't know what I'm good at."

"That's normal for orphan girls," Victoria told them. "Most kids get to try out different ideas with their parents, but we never got that. So hash them out with me. If you could be anything at all in the world, what would you be?"

"I know," Aurora said with a big smile. "I want to

fly jet fighters for the Navy!"

Victoria nodded approvingly, then looked at Nevine. Nevine thought for a moment, then said, "Maybe a scientist, particularly one that fights ghosts." It sounded stupid, even as she said it.

Victoria thought about that for a moment and smiled. "Well, Grimoire Manor is certainly the right place to get started on that!"

Chapter 9

Vysehrad Cemetery

Each night when she went to sleep, Nevine wondered where she would wake up. Once she'd gone to sleep in her bed at Grimoire and awakened in a snowy alley in Prague. Later, she'd gone to sleep in her room in the observatory and awakened back at Grimoire Manor. In between, however, as each successive night brought no change, she began to think that her current location was, more or less, permanent. As such, when she went to sleep that night after dinner with Victoria Turnbell and Aurora, she fully expected to wake up and prepare for her morning classes. Instead, her sleepy eyes were greeted with her makeshift bedroom in the observatory, with December frost glazing over her little window.

It took her a moment to fully realize what had happened. She was puzzled as to how and why this was occurring, but felt a bolt of excitement at being back in Prague with Xanthae and Petyr. Once again, she asked herself if there was any way that this could have all been a dream, but it was just too real. Besides, by now there were enough connections between Grimoire Manor and Prague for her to suspect that there was something else going on other than just her imagination.

She got dressed very quickly in some of the plain but new clothes Xanthae had bought for her and ran out into the central observatory. She found Xanthae polishing the main telescope and nearly tackled her with a hug.

"Well, good morning for you too!" Xanthae said with a little laugh.

With her mouth moving at about a hundred miles an hour, Nevine told Xanthae all about what had happened in Grimoire Manor. Only with great reluctance did she slow down to take a few breaths. Xanthae listened to it all with great interest, occasionally suggesting that she slow down a bit. At the end of the story, Xanthae had a look that was both puzzled and a bit concerned. "Well, certainly changes things this does," she said with furrowed brows. "If you are flipping back and forth between Prague and this Grimoire Manor, it must be purely a, well…" —and it was obvious Xanthae didn't like the word she was about to use— "psychic event…by which I say that these transfers involve only your mind, not any magical or supernatural process. Remember, if things happen in the natural world…"

"…then they're part of the natural world and subject to its laws," Nevine finished for her, as a good student should.

"Yes," Xanthae said, "and if we could know the laws that govern how and why you make these transitions, we may figure out what makes them occur. Caution you, I must, however, to tell no one at all about these transitions. If the Society for Metaphysical Research were to hear of them, they'd want to study you. And there's no telling what that might involve!"

Nevine shuddered instinctively.

"I think there's a connection between the Grimoire family and Prague. I think they must have lived here."

"That's certainly possible," Xanthae said. "I've never heard of them, but then again, I seldom socialize with the rich and powerful. Well, except for the mayoress' masquerade ball, which I don't know why she has honored us with that invitation. If they, the family, did live in beautiful Prague for any length of time, there might be records…birth and death records, business records…although I do not think the mayoress would be so helpful as to allow us access."

"What about Novak and Skounic?" Nevine asked, referring to the two soldiers who were also searching for the Vysehrad Ghoul.

"That mayoress' bounty, because of her, it's unlikely they'll share information with us. If this were about the Vysehrad Ghoul, think I might give them our information, anyway, as perhaps they could succeed in cornering the Ghoul. We don't have any reason to suspect that your Grimoire Ghost and the Vysehrad Ghoul are connected at all, but…" Xanthae seemed to think for a moment.

"What is it, Professor Halruaa?"

Xanthae shook her head. "It's nothing other than whenever something about your presence here seems to be just an odd coincidence, it proves to be much more relevant than we would have suspected. I'll tell you what. Petyr is still working on the flamethrower, so we may have an afternoon to do some exploring, just the two of us. Many of the rich, notable families of Prague bury their dead at the Vysehrad Cemetery, just a short walk from here. What say you about the possibility that the Grimoire family might have buried their dead there, if they lived in this city? It's the only record of their presence I can think to look for without the mayoress' help."

Nevine smiled and shrugged. "That sounds reasonable to me."

"If there was a Grimoire family tomb, that would prove a connection with your Grimoire Manor, I think. Although, I would like to know for how long they lived in Prague, and why they then moved to America. It is possible that in 1888, the Grimoire family is still here in Prague."

After breakfast, which consisted of eggs, milk and dried fruits, they decided whether there was anything they would need to bring with them. In the end, Xanthae had them each carry two flares, although she didn't say why they might be necessary during the day. Nevine noticed that she was still wearing the little diamond necklace that the mayoress had given her and asked Xanthae if it was okay for her to still wear it.

"I can see no harm in it," Xanthae said with a moment's thought, "for now."

It was still before lunch when they set out across the Vysehrad park. The day proved to be a nice one for December, with a glowing sun above, and no wind, keeping the temperature rather reasonable. There were well-worn paths through the old snow, so walking across Vysehrad was not difficult. As they went, Nevine saw the spot where the Grimoire family had taken their family portrait and pointed it out. She recognized even the tree near which they had stood.

Xanthae led Nevine past the Cathedral of Saints Paul and Peter into the Vysehrad Cemetery. This cemetery was unlike any that Nevine had seen in America. Most American cemeteries, to Nevine at least, seemed to be wide open with lots of trees and grass, and modest-sized gravestones, except perhaps for a few larger family plots. Here, there was very little grass, although a few trees were left to provide shade. The tombs were packed in close together with no room between them for grass. The tombs themselves, despite the small space provided for them, were quite ornate, with large, coffin-sized marble markers possessed of lavish decorations. Indeed, the large structures above ground made Nevine wonder if the bodies were buried below ground at all. The decorations were much more complex than those seen in American cemeteries, with elaborate angels, and sometimes skeletons, lines of poetry, signatures in the dead person's hand, even busts of the deceased's head. Candle holders hung over some of the dead, so that mourners could light a little candle of prayer. With all of these lit up at night, the cemetery would make for an impressive sight.

Some of the tombs were much larger than the others, and a few had stairways leading up, perhaps fifteen to twenty feet, to the grave markers of all the family dead. Although the markers were very large, it was not uncommon to find ten or sometimes more people buried in the same small place, which made Nevine wonder again how all the bodies were made to fit.

Along the outside of the cemetery were still more elaborate tombs. These were placed along a continuous wall, and included a little roof, so that the vaults were protected from the rain. A mourner had to pass through a little gate to get to these tombs. The ceiling of the little roof was decorated with mosaic tiles of angels or religious scenes. Candle holders and elaborate statues were once again commonplace amongst these tombs, which seemed almost fit for royalty. A single heavy-looking block was bolted to the ground at each of these tombs, which Nevine guessed marked the spot where the bodies lay.

"This is the strangest looking cemetery I've ever seen," Nevine said in total awe.

"I suppose the last thing you can buy yourself before death is a really nice grave marker," Xanthae suggested. "We should be able to read all the markers in a couple of hours if we don't dawdle, which I can see you're already tempted to do."

"It's just like this was a museum," Nevine said by way of explanation.

"Well, we live about a minute's walk away, so you come visit the dead anytime you like. From the look of these stones, I'd guess they wouldn't mind some visitors. For now, we've got to keep eyes sharp for the names. Grimoire's not a Czech name, at least, so if it's here, it should stand out."

They guessed that if the Grimoire family had the money to own expensive properties in both Prague and Newport, then they must have been rich indeed, and so they tried the outermost ring of tombs, those with the roof and mosaic tiles first. This proved to be a timely decision, for they found the Grimoire tomb as the eighth one they examined.

Like its fellows, the Grimoire tomb was an artistic masterpiece. Over the heavy plate in the ground, a smoothed granite marker detailed the names of the dead and their years of birth and death. Over this was a giant female angel, sculpted to appear as if the flowing ripples of her gown and the feathers of her spread wings were embracing the tomb and protecting it. The angel held a trumpet in one hand, and she appeared to be a young woman except that her face had an emaciated and almost frightening appearance. In the mosaic tiles on the ceiling was the image of a sunset as seen across an ocean beach, with the words "Deus Vult" in green tiles.

"Interesting choices," Xanthae commented. "There are no beaches near Prague."

"Maybe it's from France," Nevine suggested. "I think that's where they're from originally. Or maybe they've already been to Newport. What do the words mean?"

"God wills it," Xanthae said. "Ironically, those words are too often used to defend that which God doesn't want at all, like war and hatred toward others who are different from ourselves. I suppose here it's meant to imply that God has willed that we all die one day."

They were silent for a moment as they pondered the Grimoires' tomb. Nevine's mind was bothered with something…it was something she thought of from time to time, but had never had anyone to talk to about it before. Now, shyly, she asked, "What do you think happens to us when we die?"

Xanthae was still staring at the tomb. "Unfortunately, there's only one way to get a scientific answer to that question, and never having died before, I don't have that answer."

Nevine was quite unsatisfied by that reply, and when Xanthae looked over, she seemed to sense it. She came over and hugged Nevine. "Oh, well, Nevine, I think most of us probably worry about that from time and again. I wish I could tell you that I knew for certain, but I don't. If want you my opinion though, I think that the laws of nature are so beautiful, so perfect...and they didn't need to be that way you know...that it's difficult not to see some divine hand in the matter. Finding out what happens after death is one of the great mysteries of life. I'm not rushing to find the answer, but when it's time when I'm a hundred and ninety-nine years old, I think I'll be quite excited to find out. Since there's nothing we can do about it, there's no point worrying. You should only ever worry about things you have the power to change." She squeezed Nevine's shoulders gently. "Let's try to enjoy this life as best we can."

They returned their attention to the tomb. There were five names on it—all of them deceased within the last ten years. Two of the dead had been elderly, the other two were children. One had not lived even for a year; the other had been a little girl of about ten years.

"All the deaths are reasonably recent. Perhaps this Grimoire family has not been in Prague for terribly long," Xanthae observed.

"I wonder why there are as many dead children as old people?" Nevine asked.

"Well, I hate to say it," Xanthae said, "but many children die rather young. It's infectious diseases that cause the deaths mainly: influenza, measles, diphtheria, and the like."

"I think that I've been vaccinated against most of those."

"Really?" Xanthae exclaimed, quite impressed.

The fifth name was that of a young man, Thierry Grimoire, who had died only a month earlier, and whose name Nevine recognized from the portrait Aurora had found in the Grimoire Manor attic. She was about to point this out to Xanthae when from behind them in the cemetery, Nevine noticed the approach of a familiar *step, shhloooop...step, shhloooop* from the night of her arrival in Prague. Her heart seemed to come to a screeching halt, and she turned to look. There, walking through the center of Vysehrad Cemetery, was a figure with the familiar cloak, top hat, and limp of the Vysehrad Ghoul. Only now his features were not those of the horrible walking corpse that she had encountered on the streets of Prague, but rather those of a young man who might have been ill, perhaps, but otherwise weren't entirely unpleasant. She could not help but draw in a sharp breath as she realized that she recognized these features. She had seen them in the Grimoire family portrait. The name "Thierry" had been written below him.

Nervously, almost frozen in place, Nevine reached out and tugged on Xanthae's sleeve. "Hmm...yes?" Xanthae turned to Nevine and saw the look on her face. "What is it, dear?" Then she followed Nevine's gaze and saw the man too. Xanthae could not have recognized the face, but it must have come as a shock to her to realize the Ghoul now had a face, but the manner of his walk, and the hat and the cloak were unmistakable.

The Ghoul of Vysehrad...Thierry Grimoire...was quietly walking toward the tomb of his family...which was supposed to be his own final resting place. He looked up as he neared the tomb and saw Xanthae and

Nevine already waiting there, staring at him. He paused for a moment, seeming almost embarrassed; then he gave an awkward little smile, tipped his hat to them with his fingers, and turned to leave.

"That's him," Nevine whispered. "That's Thierry Grimoire! He's supposed to be dead!"

"Oh my," Xanthae said, sounding dumbfounded. "I've been so stupid." She began moving, obviously intent on intercepting Thierry Grimoire.

"We don't have any kerosene!" Nevine whispered desperately.

"We can't let him get away!" Xanthae insisted and continued her pursuit. Nevine could do nothing but follow after her.

Thierry Grimoire looked back at them. Not surprisingly, he broke into a run. He was not as fast as he had been on the night that he had attacked Nevine…the night he had truly been a ghoul. Now the injury to his leg seemed to hold him back. His limp allowed Xanthae and Nevine a good chance of catching him.

"*Arrêt*, Monsieur Grimoire!" Xanthae called after him, trying to sound non-threatening. "Wait, Thierry!" However innocent Xanthae may have tried to make herself sound this morning, she had, of course, just shot the Ghoul two nights previous, and even in his revitalized form, it was likely that he remembered this. He missed not a pace in his limping run. Xanthae and Nevine hurried after him, although, in truth, they had no plan about what to do with him if and when they caught him.

With her shorter legs, Nevine was the slowest of the three, and fell behind in their pursuit. They ran out from between the gravestones, past the Cathedral of Saints Paul and Peter and into the Vysehrad Park. There were a few other people about and, although Xanthae shouted at them in Czech, they did nothing but stop and stare. Nevine imagined the three of them chasing through the snow in Vysehrad Park must have seemed an odd spectacle.

It appeared, though revitalized, that Thierry Grimoire must have been stronger and faster in his ghoul state, for Xanthae proved to be faster than he with his limp. Nevine watched as Xanthae got her hands on his cloak and pulled him to a standstill. Perhaps she had hoped to speak with him or reason with him, but of course, he was in no mood for such a thing. Knowing he could no longer escape, he turned on Xanthae, and from the folds of his cloak he produced a long, curved knife.

Nevine felt a moment of the worst fear she had ever felt in her life, even worse than the ghosts of Grimoire Manor or being chased by the Ghoul herself. Xanthae was in danger and Nevine would give anything to exchange their places; to keep Xanthae from harm. But what could she possibly do? She had the flares that Xanthae had given her, but no kerosene. Although the Ghoul might have been afraid of the light from the flares before, he was now out during the daytime. Thierry Grimoire had the knife high above his head, the tip of it aimed for Xanthae's heart. Xanthae held up her hands as a shield, but she turned her head and yelled for Nevine to run and save herself. Nevine was desperate for anything to do, but could think of nothing. All she could think of as she ran up to them was to cry out desperately, "Stop, please!" and then she also remembered the word in Czech, for Xanthae had taught it to her, "Stůj!"

And then the most remarkable thing happened. Thierry Grimoire, his raging eyes focused on Xanthae, knife held poised to cut out her heart, suddenly stopped. For a moment, time seemed to cease altogether. Nevine came to a halt just a few feet from the two of them. Xanthae held her hands up, waiting for a strike that never came. The world seemed to become silent and crystal clear in that second, and Nevine was aware of every last thing that occurred around them, from the fast beating of the heart of a nearby bird to the smooth drip of a drop of water off the tip of a melting icicle.

Thierry Grimoire released his grip on Xanthae, and lowered the hand with the knife in it, letting it dangle loosely from his fingers. He turned and looked at Nevine with an expression that was baffled…and somehow desperate. He took a step toward her, and then dragged his limp foot, then another step. Nevine stood her ground, afraid, and yet sure somehow that this was not like the first night in Prague—he did not now want to hurt her.

Xanthae was yelling at her, yelling for her to run. She had that funny pistol out now, but she couldn't shoot because he was too close to Nevine, and the pistol was not likely to harm him very much, anyway.

Thierry Grimoire came within a foot of Nevine, and he held out his hand, the hand without the knife, toward her. This close, Nevine could see that Thierry was not perfectly revitalized. His skin had a pale pallor to it, as if he were sick, and his eyes were bloodshot with noticeable bags under them. Nevine guessed he was degrading, as the life energy he had stolen from the tall woman wore off until by the end of seven days he would be nothing again but a rotting corpse. His finger reached out and touched her cheek and she let him, although her body tried instinctively to pull away. It was a gentle touch, indeed, an oddly delicate one, though his expression remained a curious mixture of surprise and confusion. He opened his mouth, tried to speak, although all he managed was that sigh...even revitalized a ghoul could not properly speak, it seemed. His breath smelled of dirt and rotting leaves.

He turned back to look at Xanthae, who still held her gun on him, although she was now silent. Then he looked back at Nevine. Whatever he had tried to communicate, he gave up on and turned once again, moving away through the snow toward the gate of Castle Vysehrad. After a few lurching steps, he broke back into his awkward run. This time, they did not follow him. Xanthae traced his steps with her gun, but did not fire on him, and as he receded into the distance, she put her gun away. Then she rushed over to Nevine and embraced her.

"Are you all right?" Xanthae asked, her voice desperate. "Know you what happened?"

"I thought he was going to kill you!" Nevine cried, throwing her arms around Xanthae's neck. Hot tears streaked down her cheeks into Xanthae's hair.

"It is my fault." Xanthae was crying too, clutching Nevine tightly. "I put you in great danger. We should not have chased him. You were wiser than I; you knew we could not stop him!"

"No, you were right to try," Nevine insisted in return. "We couldn't just let him get away again. He'll kill somebody else when he becomes a ghoul again, won't he?"

They sat in the snow, exhausted. Xanthae looked as tired as Nevine felt, and Nevine certainly needed to catch her breath. "I've been such a fool," Xanthae said. "I should have guessed what would happen when he stole the life force of his victims. Their life force enables him to return to the human form he had before death...but only for a while. He must feed regularly to maintain that form. I wonder why, though...why did he do as you asked? He seemed almost kind to you. He was ready to kill you just two nights before."

"I wonder why he was returning to his family tomb?" Nevine wiped a last tear from her eyes. "Could it be that there is a crypt under there, and that's where he sleeps?"

"I wonder..." Xanthae gave Nevine another hug and then stood up. "You are the bravest young woman I have ever known, Nevine, and you have saved my life twice now. Since we've only known each other for three days, that makes me seem very careless. I think, though, that the Ghoul...Thierry Grimoire...will not return to the cemetery in the next few hours. He'll have to soon, though, as he burns away his victim's life force and becomes a ghoul once more. He won't be able to tolerate the light then." Xanthae thought for a moment. "Unless, of course, he can find another dark place to hide during the day. Will you come with me for a moment? I wish to have another look at the Grimoire family tomb."

The adrenaline from the chase slowly seeped out of them as they made their way back to the cemetery. Nevine was feeling oddly lightheaded and confused. She was thinking about the way the Ghoul had looked at her, not at all like the heartless monster who stole people's lives and turned them into ghouls. Rather, he had seemed oddly sad...and even affectionate.

Acting on Nevine's theory that perhaps there was a crypt under the Grimoire family tomb, they carefully searched over the tomb and grave marker. Xanthae reasoned that if the Ghoul were using it to sleep during the days, particularly as his revitalization wore off, then there must be some easy way of gaining access, a hidden release or button, perhaps. Try as they did, they could not find one.

"Could we just pry open the burial cover?" Nevine asked.

"It would take several strong men to do that," Xanthae said, frowning, "and we'd need to get official permission. Perhaps we could speak with Novak and Skounic, but...the truth is that our only evidence that Thierry Grimoire is the ghoul is that you recognized him from a picture you saw in Newport. That won't be enough for private citizens such as ourselves to convince the authorities to start ripping open the tombs of notable citizens."

"What are we going to do, then?" Nevine asked, feeling frustrated herself.

Xanthae thought for a moment, and then a smile crossed her face. "Know you this...I think I have an idea!"

Chapter 10

The Masquerade Ball

Nevine and Xanthae had much to talk about and also much to do that afternoon. They returned briefly to the observatory, where they told a shocked Petyr what had occurred. They also picked up some supplies for Xanthae's plan, which consisted mainly of several small metal buttons and a long length of very thin wire. This time, Petyr accompanied them back to the tomb, carrying several glass vials of kerosene in case the Ghoul returned.

"It's possible that the Ghoul won't come back to this location," Xanthae said as they walked through the snow, "now that he knows we're aware of his hiding place. He may find another place to hide during the day as his body further corrodes. I think that he must try to hold off feeding as long as he can, but the urge becomes more unbearable the further he decays. If the Ghoul does come back to this tomb, however, I want to know about it."

They tried to search once again, with Petyr helping this time, for any secret latch that might have opened the tomb to reveal the crypt they suspected was hidden underneath. Once again, they had no luck. Failing at that, they carefully positioned one set of the little metal buttons over the plate on the floor of the tomb, and the other set just next to the grave marker. The buttons were very small and placed so they were hidden and difficult to find. The buttons were attached to the thin wire, and this was strung back to the observatory. They took great care to make sure the wire was carefully buried underneath the snow and not visible to anyone. Back at the observatory, the wire was connected to a little electrical bell, which was powered by their river-driven generator.

"What we have done," explained Xanthae, "is effectively set up something like a small telegraph machine. Should the tomb plate be opened, or the grave marker be moved, this will cause the little buttons to touch one another. This will complete an electrical circuit, which will cause the bell to ring. Once it is activated, this bell will continue ringing until we deactivate it. That way, we will be able to know the Ghoul has returned, even if we are not home at the time. A telegraph machine uses electrical currents in much the same way, to send coded signals across miles and miles of wire. Know you why the wire is coated with rubber?" she asked Nevine.

"It's to keep you from getting zapped if you touch it?" Nevine guessed.

Nevine had to explain what 'zapped' meant to Xanthae and Petyr, but once she understood, Xanthae laughed. "That's somewhat true, although I wouldn't test it. The rubber does not conduct electricity very well, so it helps the electric charge stay in the wire, rather than jumping out into the ground or someone touching the wire. Given a choice, electricity usually wants to travel into the ground in the quickest way possible. You always want to be sure you're not the quickest way. If the voltage of the wire is very high, or there is a lot of push behind the current, the electricity can pass through insulators. Say, for instance, you touched a high-voltage wire while standing on the ground. The electrical current wants to go into the ground, and if there is enough power behind the current, it could go through the rubber, into your hand, through your body, and into the ground. Naturally, this could do you great harm or potentially kill you, so I recommend that you take my word for it on this."

Returning to the observatory, they were all excited about the possibility that the bell might ring and they would have their quarry. That afternoon and evening, the three of them remained in the observatory waiting for the Ghoul's return. Petyr spent his time working on the flamethrower; by this time he had a working model which he was testing for its propulsion ability with ordinary water, producing what Nevine figured was the best super-soaker she had ever seen. Xanthae and Nevine worked on some lessons, physics at first, then some Czech, although finally the talk turned to ghost-hunting. Nevine, in particular, was eager for advice on what to do with the Hallway Ghost.

"I should caution you," Xanthae said, taking her motherly tone, "on attempting to interfere with this spirit on your own. I know very well that you'll ignore me, though, so I'll give you what information I can. Let me start by telling you that in my experience, apparitions come in four main types. It's possible perhaps that there are others, but these are the four that I have seen.

"The first is a phantom. This type of apparition typically never leaves a particular room or hallway.

Usually, it is the scene of some tragic event, a murder perhaps, or suicide. The phantom replays the moment of the tragedy over and over again through time with no variations. It is always the same regardless of who may or may not be witnessing it. Phantoms do not react to others who are present and essentially appear to be mindless. My belief is that phantoms are the result of some form of electromagnetic 'scarring' that occurs in the environment due to the tortured mental state of the victim, sort of like how bright light would leave an image behind on a photograph. So a phantom is more akin to a photograph rather than a trapped soul of any sort and they tend to fade over time."

Nevine nodded, intrigued.

"The second apparition you may come across is what some have called a poltergeist. Typically, this focuses on one person and will follow that person across locations. Often the person is a youth who is very sad or angry. The poltergeist is typically recognized by the throwing of objects, particularly when such objects may harm others. The poltergeist is typically not a true haunting, but is the result of the person's own anger…it is the youth who is causing the damage to be done, not a ghost. Somehow, the person's emotions are so strong that they affect the electromagnetic forces in the room and can make things move in unpredictable ways. The person may not even be aware they are doing it or that they are responsible, and may think they are haunted."

Nevine was listening intently.

"It is the other two that are more relevant to what you have described to me. The next apparition is the typical ghost. What we could call a ghost is a true soul that has failed to cut its ties with the material world. As with phantoms, many ghosts seem to originate under tragic conditions, although this is not always the case. Ghosts do seem to have awareness and may interact with observers, although in my experience, they will only do so when forced. Confronting your Hallway Ghost on your first night at this Grimoire Manor may have been enough to provoke it. Ghosts may repeat the same actions over and over, although this may involve interactions with the physical world. In my observations, ghosts seem to have difficulty passing through barriers that are poor electrical conductors, such as wooden doors, which makes me think that ghosts use some form of electromagnetic force to manipulate objects.

"Now, technically, most of the interactions we see between forms of matter on a day-to-day basis are electromagnetic. When I touch you," —Xanthae put her hand on Nevine's shoulder— "the molecules in my body exert electromagnetic forces on the molecules in your body that, in the case of stable molecules, generally repel each other, no offense…this essentially is what keeps us from falling through the floor or my hand from passing through your shoulder. Ghosts manage to do more or less the same thing, perhaps by manipulating the electromagnetic qualities of air molecules, although I am not sure how they do this. As you might expect, the forces that ghosts can exert tend to be quite weak, although they can be quite frightening because they are unexpected."

"So tell me," Nevine asked, "what's the difference between a ghost and a phantom?"

"Both seem to be comprised of electromagnetic

radiation, not matter like you and me. However, a phantom will not interact with you because it has no mind, whereas a ghost will interact. It's kind of like the difference between a photograph of Nevine Turner and the real Nevine Turner. Does that make sense?"

"I think so," Nevine said, absorbing it all.

"Lastly, we have a class similar to ghosts that I have termed specters. Like ghosts, these apparitions tend to haunt a particular location and stay near to it. Unlike ghosts, specters appear to be less often created by a specific tragedy, and more often by an accumulation of misdeeds. As such, specters are less likely to be attempting to 'solve' a tragic event and are more likely to attempt to avoid divine judgment. Specters are more likely than ghosts to interact, often quite violently with observers, and seem to be capable of exerting stronger electromagnetic forces. I would avoid specters if at all possible."

Nevine considered everything Xanthae had told her. "I think the Hallway Ghost sounds like just that…a ghost…although the thing in the attic…could that have been a specter?"

"It is difficult for me to be certain without actually witnessing them myself, but I suspect you are correct. This means, of course, that there are at least two apparitions at Grimoire Manor. I would avoid the specter until we have much more opportunity to train you. As for the ghost, if there is to be any hope of releasing it from its torment, we must understand what event caused the ghost to become stuck to the location in the first place. If the event is something that you may be able to remedy, you may be able to free the ghost. If the event can not be remedied, there may be little that you can do. Be aware that while ghosts are typically not aggressive, they can become so if extremely provoked."

****

Despite their excitement, the bell that was hooked up to the Grimoire family tomb did not ring that day or that evening. By the next day, they had to admit that it was likely the Ghoul of Vysehrad had sought shelter elsewhere. Their only other recourse was to attempt to find out as much as they could about the Grimoire family, even though it was unlikely they would get much assistance from the mayoress or her bureaucrats.

Nevine actually enjoyed the next few days, as they involved spending lots of time with Xanthae alone walking through the streets of Prague in their quest for information. The city was really quite beautiful, and Xanthae made sure they visited some of the finer points of the city. They walked through Prague Castle and explored the Cathedral of St. Vitus. Here, they walked up the steps of the Main Tower, which was no easy task, as hundreds and hundreds of stone steps circled around and around each other in a tight coil, and Nevine was out of breath by the time they got to the top. The tower provided a breathtaking view of Prague, however, and was well worth it.

They dined at several eateries along the Vltava River and sometimes stopped on their walks to listen to street musicians play. Between all of this, they found out some information on the Grimoires, but not much. What they discovered was that the Grimoire family was French, which was not a surprise, and had moved to Prague twenty years earlier in connection to some business opportunities that had gone very well and made the family quite wealthy. In recent years, those businesses had begun to decline, and the Grimoires had left for America six months previously.

Petyr managed to finish the flamethrower and do so without setting himself on fire, which pleased Xanthae very much. The bell never rang, and so they concluded it was unlikely that the Vysehrad Ghoul would return to the Grimoire family tomb. Nevine could see that Xanthae was frustrated by this, as it was nearly time for the Ghoul to feed again, and they would have failed in saving the life of the Ghoul's next victim.

Toward the end of that week, the time for the Mayoress' Masquerade Ball arrived, and with mixed feelings, they dressed themselves once again in their finest clothes, and set off in a rented coach for Prague Castle, where the ball was being held. Their masks covered only the upper parts of their faces, so it was not like Halloween, really (Xanthae had never heard of Halloween, and Nevine had to explain it to her). There were no elaborate costumes, and it was not difficult to tell who was who. Nevertheless, Nevine's mask had whiskers like a cat, and Xanthae's feathers were like a bird, which rather went with her wild hair. Petyr had chosen a mask with a black-and-white checkered pattern, which he said was Venetian. Cleaned up and dressed elegantly, he was rather fetching, Nevine thought.

There were already many people at the ball when they arrived—men, women, and children, all dressed in elegant clothing and masks. A few people had masks which did cover the whole face and it was impossible to know who they were. There were tables of food laid out, and a floor for dancing. A small orchestra played waltzes and other dances, and several couples were already on the floor. Other people stood around in small groups talking about all manner of things. Waiters in suits carried trays of wine and water.

"Look," Nevine said, quite impressed. "Is that a fountain of chocolate?" She pointed to a fountain set in one corner that sprang forth with brown liquids. Numerous children were dipping little cakes and fruits into the fountain. Wow, how long had it been since she had eaten chocolate, Nevine wondered.

"Either that or the Prague sewers have backed up again," Petyr joked. Xanthae slapped him on the shoulder.

"I should probably make you eat a vegetable or something first, but…well, don't get too far from me," Xanthae warned. "I don't trust this at all. I don't know what the mayoress might be up to."

"So suspicious," Petyr replied jokingly, although there was a tone to his voice suggesting that he actually agreed. "Who needs a reason to have a party?"

Nevine gave Xanthae a reassuring wave and moved off to the fountain. Dipping a cake into the chocolate, she found it bitterer than she had expected, but still delicious. She was enjoying herself when she noticed a man in a white soldier's uniform was standing next to her.

"Well, Miss Nevine Turner," the soldier Novak said to her, his voice friendly, "it is quite a pleasure to find you here. The chocolate does look good, but at my age, one must be careful to not eat too much." Novak patted his belly, which was perhaps a tad round, although not so bad as he seemed to think.

Nevine instinctively looked for Xanthae, and noticed the other soldier, Skounic, was talking with her.

They both looked quite serious, and Nevine wondered if they were arguing. Petyr had moved off into the crowd and it looked as if he had found a young lady to waltz with him. Nevine felt a pang of disapproval, although it was a rather silly reaction.

Nevine looked up at Novak and said apologetically through a mouthful of cake, "I think that we're in competition with each other."

Novak nodded. "Yes, and that's too bad. We should be helping each other catch the Ghoul. Still, competition can sometimes be good. My partner, Skounic, is quite excited about the bounty. I'm probably cheating by asking you this, but I wonder, had you any luck in tracking the Ghoul?"

Nevine looked over at Xanthae, who was still discussing something with Skounic. Nevine considered mentioning the Grimoire Tomb to Novak, but decided it would be best to let Xanthae say anything that needed mentioning. So she shook her head.

"That is too bad." He patted Nevine on the shoulder. "Well, don't give up hope. One of us will catch him sooner or later."

"What would you do with the bounty if you and Mr. Skounic get it?" Nevine asked.

"I don't know," Novak replied, putting his hand to his chin as he thought for a moment. "Pay off a few debts, I suppose. Perhaps put a little money aside for when I become too old for soldiering."

"Do you have a family?"

Novak smiled, but shook his head a bit sadly. "No, I'm sorry to say that I don't. I was married for many years, but my wife got consumption and died some years ago. I had a boy who went into the army, but he died as well, so I'm on my own now."

"Me too," Nevine said. "I never knew my mom or dad. Xanthae's been the only parent I have ever known."

"Well, you're lucky to have her take you on. She's as brilliant as any man I've ever known." Nevine wasn't sure what that meant exactly, since all the girls she knew seemed much smarter than boys to her, but it sounded like he meant it as a compliment. "Well then," he said, "I'll leave you to your feasting. Enjoy the ball."

Nevine had filled herself on pastries and cakes; in fact, she was regretting not leaving the fountain behind her a little sooner than she did, but who could be blamed for overdoing it with a chocolate fountain? She looked over at Xanthae, who was now talking to a very handsome man with graying temples, who was clearly an admirer. Xanthae looked less admiring, wearing the same scowl she had since entering the ballroom. As Nevine watched, the man seemed to reach out to touch Xanthae's face, but she leaned back and practically swatted his hand away. The man looked apologetic, but Nevine was unable to see more of what happened, for she bumped into a tall, thin man whose mask covered his whole face.

The man turned around to face her in the tottering, deliberate manner of an elderly person. "Ah," he said, looking down, *"Dobrý večer."* His voice was kind, and it sounded like 'doebrEE veCHER.' It meant 'good evening,' which Nevine remembered from her lessons.

"Dobrý večer," she replied with a little courtesy. *"Mluvíte anglicky? Mluvím jen trochu česky."* She had told him that she spoke only a little Czech and asked if he spoke English.

"Ah, must you be this Nevine Turner I have been hearing about?" he replied in excellent, although accented, English.

"You've been hearing about me?" Nevine asked, scrunching her face, puzzled. She was not used to being the focus of attention. Mostly during her years in foster care, she had gotten used to feeling unnoticed.

"Oh yes," the man said, "I've heard that you were very brave in fighting the ghouls that have plagued our city. My name is Dalek Viliček and I am a doctor. Perhaps would care you to share a waltz with an old man?"

Nevine felt a bit uncertain about that. "I don't know how to waltz."

"It's quite simple." He showed her how to step to the three-part beat of the music. "And I'll be honest and say that most people will expect only little things from an old man and a young American, so we can only hope to impress them."

Indeed, once they were on the dance floor, she found the waltz relatively easy to pick up once she got the three-step routine down. "What kind of doctor are you?" Nevine asked once they were among the dancing couples.

"Oh, I'm not a doctor of people." The old man laughed. "I am a doctor of the stars and the planets."

"Like Professor Halruaa," Nevine said.

"Yes," Viliček replied. "Our fields overlap quite a bit, although Professor Halruaa and I differ in outlook at times. Still, I am a great admirer of hers, and you have been most fortunate to find yourself in the care of such an exemplary person."

"I know. She's been great and I've learned a lot."

"What a beautiful necklace you have," Viliček exclaimed, noticing the little diamond around her neck. "Was that given to you by Professor Halruaa?"

A little warning bell sounded in her head for some reason, but ultimately she could find no reason for not telling the truth. "No, it was the mayoress who gave this to me."

The old man let out a pleasant little laugh. "Well, you certainly have made quite an impression on many people for such a short time in Prague."

Nevine looked up at him, curious. "How do you know how long I have been in Prague?"

"Oh, well, that." Viliček drew in a long breath. "I have made it my life's work to study all manner of extraordinary phenomena and I think that you are one of the most extraordinary of them all."

There was a moment's pause as Nevine thought about what he had said. Then the song ended and the dancers broke apart. "Thank you very much for dancing with me," Viliček said kindly. "You have been an excellent dancing companion, but an old man such as myself has only one dance in him. Besides, I suspect your guardian is beckoning you."

"You're welcome, Dr. Viliček," she replied, and noticed at that moment that Xanthae was indeed watching them, and did not look pleased. Nevine ran over to Xanthae and asked what the matter was.

"Do you remember when I told you about the Society for Metaphysical Research?" Xanthae said.

"Yes, you said they do very bad things because they fear dying."

"That's correct. Well, Dr. Viliček is among their members. He once was a prominent scientist." There was a hint of sadness in Xanthae's voice. "Although his interests turned to necromancy."

"What's that?" Nevine asked.

"Necromancy is a study of magic and is most evil and satanic. Necromancy interferes with the natural laws of life, speaking with the dead, causing corpses to rise from the grave, and seeking to extend the natural life by stealing life from others. It is the subject that unites the members of the Society for Metaphysical Research as they seek to extend their lives at the cost to others, and indeed even their own souls."

Nevine shuddered, finding it hard to believe that the kind old man with whom she had danced could be involved in something so evil. "I'm sorry, I didn't know that he was bad."

Xanthae patted her shoulder gently. "You're not at fault. I should have been more careful in warning you. I would keep my distance from that man, if you can. I know not what his interest in you might be."

At last, the mayoress found them. She was dressed in a long golden gown, and unlike her guests, wore no mask. "Good evening to you both," she said, her eyes looking them over carefully. "I am very pleased that you were able to join us."

"Good evening," Nevine said, and Xanthae said it last of all, struggling to summon up some civility. If Xanthae seemed to be uncomfortable or even hostile, the mayoress took no notice of it.

"You both look quite lovely." The mayoress smiled, although, as before, the smile held no warmth. "I have with me the documents that you want." One of the mayoress' assistants, standing just behind her, handed her a package, which she now handed to

Xanthae. "You'll find that the documents assign you full guardianship of Nevine Turner, Professor Halruaa. You'll wish to read the documents over quite closely."

Xanthae took the package. "Thank you for this act of kindness. I suppose that I am now in your debt." From the expression on her face, it was obvious she did not like being in debt to the mayoress one bit.

"If you are successful in destroying the Ghoul of Vysehrad, your debt to this city will be paid," the mayoress said, quite reasonably.

"Do you know Thierry Grimoire?" Nevine asked impulsively.

There was a pause as the mayoress looked down at her with a curious and icy expression. "I know everyone of importance in this city. I'm not at liberty to gossip about them. It would be unseemly for a woman in my position."

"Why have you invited us to this?" Xanthae asked, her voice barely above a whisper.

The mayoress hesitated, thinking for a moment. "I believe it was Sun Tzu who once said, 'To know your enemy you must become your enemy…keep your friends close and your enemies closer.' I haven't yet decided which you are. Now, if you'll excuse me, I have other guests to attend to." She turned without a further word and was gone in the crowd.

Sensing that her mentor could use it, Nevine put her hand in Xanthae's and squeezed it. Xanthae looked down and smiled at her. "What do you think, Nevine? Had we enough fun for tonight?"

Nevine nodded.

"Let's find Petyr then." Xanthae sighed. "He'll be found either where there is food or pretty girls or be any place where books are not."

****

Back at the observatory, they shrugged off their coats and settled into the comforts of familiar surroundings. They were all tired and thinking about bed.

"So what did you think of the mayoress' ball?" Xanthae asked them. She was opening the package the mayoress had given her and reading through the papers within.

"It was kind of fun," Nevine said, and it had been, despite some of the odd characters there. "I would go again." She wanted to ask Xanthae about the man she had seen her with, but didn't want to do so in front of Petyr in case it was something private.

"Well," Xanthae said, conceding the point, "perhaps I have been too judgmental. The mayoress has been true to her word with the guardianship papers."

"I met the most beautiful woman tonight." Petyr launched into a description of his adventures with potential female admirers. Nevine tried her best to ignore him but found herself getting angry. Women were not playthings to be bragged about like toys!

"Well look at this!" Xanthae exclaimed after a minute, interrupting Petyr just as Nevine was about to say something. They all rushed over to examine a paper that Xanthae held up.

"It looks like an admission record to Charles Asylum," Petyr said after examining the document for a moment. "It's a place for the insane and demented," he told Nevine.

"It was in with the guardianship papers?" Nevine asked, feeling a moment's excitement. If this was

147

something the mayoress had given them, it might very well be important.

"Yes," Xanthae said with a shocked look on her face. "The mayoress has slipped this to us. Did you notice the name on the record?"

"Thierry Grimoire!" Petyr said, and they all looked from one to the other, knowing this was a crucial piece of information, but not sure what it meant.

Suddenly, a loud ringing in the observatory startled them. Nevine felt a moment of confusion and fright before Xanthae got a look of clarification and stood up. "The Grimoire family tomb!" she exclaimed. "Someone has opened it!"

Chapter 11

Black Sun

Hastily, they prepared to investigate the Grimoire family tomb. Petyr donned his new flamethrower, which consisted of two tanks of kerosene and pressurized carbon dioxide he carried over his shoulders like a backpack, a hose, and a nozzle with a trigger and methane burner. Nevine observed that Petyr looked both excited and nervous about the possibility of actually using it. He also wore protective glasses and thick gloves to protect his hands. Xanthae and Nevine each took three flares, and Xanthae took her pistol and a vial of oil of vitriol, which she explained would be used to damage the locking mechanism of the tomb if they found it open. Nevine was tasked with carrying a small lantern, which would provide longer light than the flares.

With all of that taken care of, and their coats back on, they made the walk across Vysehrad Park to the cemetery and the tomb. There was light snow falling, and the soft sound of the flakes descending through the tree branches only emphasized the silence of the night.

Until they were close, the Grimoire family tomb looked much the same as when they had left it last. Only when they approached more closely did they see that the plate on the tomb floor had been released by some trigger, and now stood propped open just an inch or so.

Xanthae took care to look around them, saying, "We must be suspicious that the Ghoul has returned after so many days away. Surely, he must have decayed enough that he would have sought shelter before now. Always be sure to watch behind you as well as in front of you."

"Think you it could be a trap?" Petyr asked.

Xanthae nodded. "I think that it could be, although…" Xanthae examined the triggers they had left and found them undisturbed. "…I wonder if the trap is for us." Carefully, Petyr opened the floor plate all the way. "I think you find there are spring-loaded hinges that should make easy the task," Xanthae speculated.

Petyr pulled the doorway open, which revealed a set of plain stone stairs that led downward into darkness. Xanthae found the door's latch, and poured the oil of vitriol on it, producing a cloud of vapor which hissed as the latch was dissolved. She instructed them to be careful not to breathe the vapor. The plate on the floor of the tomb would be impossible to lock shut now.

Xanthae lit one of her flares and held it up. "Petyr, this would be a good time to prepare the flamethrower."

Petyr twisted a valve on the methane burner and Nevine heard a soft hiss as it began releasing methane. Xanthae dipped the flare into this methane stream, which erupted in a short blue flame. The burning methane flame crossed in front of the flamethrower nozzle. When Petyr triggered the nozzle, kerosene would be projected by the pressurized carbon dioxide across the methane flame and erupt into long bursts of burning liquid.

With the flamethrower ready, Xanthae threw the flare down the stairs where it cast its bright red glow. From where they stood, they could see only that the flare revealed the stone floor, perhaps twenty feet below. There was no movement in response to the flare. "If something is down there, it is already expecting us," Xanthae said, "and the darkness will only give it further advantage."

Petyr was the first down the stairs, followed by Xanthae, and then Nevine. They went down carefully not to trip, fully prepared for any ambush. The main room of the crypt was larger than they had been expecting. Six tall columns held up the rocky ceiling, and there were torch sconces on each of the pillars. Between the columns were five separate sarcophagi, one for each of the people buried in the crypt. Each person had been laid to rest in a large stone box with an elaborate marble cover. Two of these large marble covers had been shoved roughly aside, exposing the contents of the sarcophagi. Brass plates identified each of the dead. The sarcophagi that had been disturbed belonged to Thierry Grimoire and to a little girl of about ten who had died nearly a year earlier. Nevine set the lantern down next to one of the pillars, where it could provide the best light.

Xanthae and Nevine examined Thierry's sarcophagus, with Xanthae holding the lit flare so they could see inside. It was empty.

Petyr examined the other open grave using the methane burner for light. "There's a little girl in this one," he said. "Looks like she's been dead a year, all right. Not much left but bones and hair."

"Why would the Ghoul have opened that grave?"

Nevine wondered aloud.

Xanthae chewed on her lip, thinking for a moment. "Burn her, just in case."

Petyr took several steps back from the sarcophagus, and then squeezed a short burst of flaming kerosene into the concrete box where the little girl had been laid to rest. The concrete sarcophagi glowed with an orange flame that helped light the room further. Inside, the kerosene crackled and hissed, and there were occasional pops as bones cracked from the heat of the burning fluid. Smoke from the fire rose to the ceiling and then out the trapdoor they had left open.

"Had we closed the trapdoor," Xanthae quietly said to Nevine, "the fire would quickly consume the oxygen in the room and fill it with smoke instead, which would be quite bad for us. Most fires need oxygen to burn; without the oxygen, the fire would go out, but we would be dead as well!"

Xanthae used the lit flare to light the torches that had been left in the sconces, and with that done, the room was quite well lit. "These torches are rather new," Xanthae observed.

"Why does a ghoul that hates light need new torches, I wonder?" Nevine asked.

Xanthae smiled at her, the first time she had smiled since leaving the observatory. "That is just the sort of question a ghost hunter should be asking. Very good, Nevine. Unfortunately, we don't have an immediate answer."

They moved a little further into the crypt and found that toward the back there was a passageway that led down and north, away from the Vysehrad Cemetery and toward the city of Prague.

"This is already quite big for a crypt," Petyr observed, "and now it even has a passageway out?"

"We must be very careful," Xanthae said, "and be prepared for the unexpected."

"Professor Halruaa," Petyr asked, curiously, "how does one prepare for the unexpected? After all, if one is preparing for something, doesn't that imply that it is expected?"

"Oh, do shut up!" Xanthae hissed.

With the crackling of burning kerosene sounding behind them, they slowly moved down the passageway. Petyr was first again, with Xanthae close behind. Nevine brought up the rear of the little group and it was her job to keep watching behind them in case anyone or anything tried to sneak up on them.

It was while keeping a close eye behind them that Nevine found a little symbol etched into the stone wall of the passageway. At its center was a thick ball surrounded by two concentric circles. From the center ball radiated out twelve zigzagging rays, like the rays of the sun, which stopped at the furthest concentric circle. "Look here," Nevine cried, "I've found something."

The three of them looked the symbol over for several minutes. Finally, Xanthae said, "It's a black sun. The symbol originates in old Germanic pagan religions, and is now used in some occult practices." She thought for a moment more. "A ghoul would not bother to leave something like this."

"So someone alive made this!" Nevine said.

"I think so." Xanthae nodded sadly. "Come, we should see what other mysteries this passageway reveals to us."

Nevine was still fascinated by the little symbol,

though. Touching it with her fingers, she guessed it was relatively recent, carved into the stone within the last few weeks or so. Taking time to look more at that symbol separated her from the other two by a small distance. All at once, there was a sound like metal grinding against stone, which startled Nevine out of her observation. Between Nevine and her friends, a barred iron gate came crashing down with a loud bang.

They all rushed to it at once. It was an old iron gate, quite rusted, but very heavy. The three of them tried pulling at it, but it would not budge.

Xanthae growled something in Czech and then said, "I think we triggered this by stepping on a loose stone in the floor. There must be a latch or trigger used to raise it. We should look around for something."

They looked and looked and looked, but there was nothing they could find that would raise the gate again. Nevine was quite frightened and didn't like being separated from her friends at all. "Is this the trap?" she asked, her voice trembling.

Xanthae shook her head. "I don't think so. I'm beginning to suspect this passageway connects with the city sewers. This gate must be meant to prevent people from going further up into the crypt. I don't think that any of us are trapped, but I don't like us being separated from you at all."

"Me either!" Nevine agreed.

"It will be better for us to stay here while you search for a lever or crank that may raise this gate. That way, if you run into trouble, you can run back here to us and we can protect you with the pistol or flamethrower."

"Shout if you have any trouble!" Petyr said with an

encouraging smile.

Nevine nodded in agreement. "I think I might know where the lever may be."

"Test your hypothesis then," Xanthae instructed her, "and hurry back here at once, whether it works or not. And keep speaking so that we know you are all right!"

Feeling quite unsure about things, Nevine ran back up the passageway into the crypt. By now, the fire in the little girl's sarcophagus had died out. This was quite fortunate, as it was here that Nevine suspected the lever for the gate might have been hidden. It would explain why the lid of the sarcophagus had been pushed off.

She wasn't able to test her hypothesis immediately, as she was interrupted by a voice from above. A man's voice was calling out in Czech as a figure began coming down the stairs. Nevine froze, hiding behind a column as she watched the figure descend. When he had reached the floor of the crypt, she could see that it was Skounic, and he had his pistol drawn.

"Mr. Skounic!" Nevine called to him, and the man looked at her in surprise.

"Miss Nevine Turner," he said, "what on earth are you doing down here?"

Glad to have some help, Nevine rushed to his side, tugging at his sleeve. "Professor Halruaa and Petyr are down here as well. There's a passageway to the north, and they have been caught behind a heavy iron gate."

Skounic pressed his lips together and frowned. "All right. You will stay right here in this room. I'll see if I can help them raise the gate." He patted Nevine on the shoulder and moved away toward the north.

"Wait" Nevine turned toward him. "I think there

might be a lever in this room to raise the gate." It would have been quite useful information for Skounic had great danger not already been present. It was unfortunate too that in turning to speak with Skounic, she turned her back on the stairway above. As such, she did not see the shadowy figure in a cloak and top hat descend the stairs.

Nevine's first awareness of the danger came as she was pushed roughly aside. She lost her balance and went stumbling toward one of the stone sarcophagi. She tried to put her hands up to guard herself, but was not quick enough. Instead, she crashed head-first into the stone box. Great pain erupted at once, and it seemed as if her ability to control her legs was lost. Sliding down the side of the sarcophagus, she put a hand to her head and felt blood there. She looked up, but her vision was blurry and her head seemed to hurt even worse as she saw the light from the torches.

She was able to see Skounic turn, however, and heard him shout. His arm was raised toward the Ghoul and he fired his pistol once and then again. The Ghoul continued without stopping, descending upon Skounic without a sound. Nevine's last image of Skounic was blurred out by the Ghoul's immense black cape, and she heard him scream with pain and terror.

She watched as the floor appeared to rush up at her, even her arms feeling as though made of lead. Her eyes struggled to close as waves of exhaustion swept over her, as if closing her eyes, all the pain in her head would go away. Hard as she tried, her eyelids fluttered one last time and then closed, and darkness welcomed her.

Chapter 12

The Bridge Between Newport and Prague

Nevine came to slowly, aware of a soft light shining on her eyes, and the distant sound of roaring. She sat up sharply and with great alarm, knowing she had been knocked unconscious by the Ghoul of Vysehrad. It took her a moment to realize that the light that had awoken her came from the early morning sun, not the torches of the crypt, and the roaring sound came from the waves crashing on the rocks of the Newport shore. She was back at Grimoire Manor. She looked around her room and saw Aurora getting ready for class.

"Oh my goodness," she said, her eyes wide. "This is not good at all."

Nevine quickly got ready, telling Aurora about her adventures as she did so.

"Oh no!" Aurora said at the end of it all. "What an awful time to flip back over here!"

It was true. Nevine felt like she had back when she was living in a particularly nasty foster home. Her case worker at that time, a nice young lady, although Nevine had long since forgotten her name, had come very close to getting Nevine adopted. There were several days where the potential family had been making up their minds. Those had been very tense days, even for a six-year-old, as she wondered if she might finally have a family. She had known that the course of her life hung in the balance. Ultimately, the family had decided not to adopt and Nevine had been crushed. The anxiety she felt now was like that…except now her life hung in the balance in a very different way. Here, in Grimoire Manor, she felt fine; there was not even a scratch on her head or a trace of a headache. Yet in Prague, she might be seconds from death.

It was not a surprise that her attention to her studies that day was poor. This was particularly true in the first-period history class. Ms. Donitz became enraged at Nevine's lackluster performance and cracked a ruler into splinters against Nevine's desk while shouting at her to pay attention.

Nevine couldn't pay attention, though, not in that class or any other. She didn't know what was going to happen to her in Prague, and what this would mean for her at Grimoire Manor. If she were killed in Prague, would she die in Newport as well? She felt, somehow, that she would…that even if her body in Newport didn't show the effects of the injuries she sustained in Prague, her soul, split from the body, would not be able to make the flip back to Newport. Of course, that was just a feeling and she couldn't be sure. She was really confused.

There was little to be done about it now, though. She could only prepare herself as best she could until she inevitably and unpredictably flipped back to Prague for her confrontation with the Vysehrad Ghoul…which might turn out to be rather quick and nasty. Until then, the only thing she could hope to achieve was to find out more information about the Hallway Ghost.

With that in mind, at the end of the day, Nevine approached Ms. Emily in the hall and asked if she could speak with her for a few minutes. Ms. Emily had to check on Joshua, who was just being dropped off from his school, but invited Nevine to come back to her apartment for a moment.

Nevine sat on a couch in the apartment, with Ms. Emily across from her in a chair. Joshua was in his room, silently playing the odd little games that he liked to play. As Nevine had expected, Joshua had not even noticed she was there, and barely even acknowledged his mother. Ms. Emily patiently fixed him a snack, offering Nevine a sandwich. At last, with Joshua taken care of, Ms. Emily asked Nevine what was on her mind.

"I wanted to ask you what you know about the Grimoire family that used to own this house."

"Well," —Ms. Emily thought— "obviously, they were very rich. They built the house in the late 1880s and owned the house through the early 1970s. At that point, the last of the Grimoires died, and the house passed to the state, as there was no one left to manage the estate. Since then, it has been the Home for Orphaned Girls that we have all come to know and love." Ms. Emily gave her a little wink.

Nevine frowned. "That's one thing I don't understand. When Aurora and I were in the attic," — her voice dropped a little, feeling awkward talking about her own rule-breaking— "we saw a picture of the last Grimoires that said it was taken in 1972. There was a little boy in the picture. How come they say the Grimoire family was all dead in the 1970s when there was still a little boy?" The question was off-topic from what Nevine really needed to know, but it seemed important nonetheless.

"Nevine, sometimes even young children die, tragic although it may be," Ms. Emily answered vaguely. Nevine said nothing, only watching Ms. Emily with an unsatisfied expression. After a moment, Ms. Emily sighed. "Fine, since you're intent on having the whole story, I suppose it's better than having you break back into the attic to try to find out. You have to understand that I wasn't even alive myself back then, so I don't know how true this is. However, when I was a resident here, some of the girls said that the last man who owned this house killed his wife and little boy and then killed himself."

Ms. Emily stopped to gauge Nevine's reaction and after a moment said, "I don't know whether to be relieved or concerned by how well you seem to have taken that."

"It makes sense," Nevine said. "I mean, it explains things, I guess."

"Does it?" Ms. Emily said testily, although Nevine guessed it wasn't due to anything that she had said, exactly. Ms. Emily gazed out of the window as if she had difficulty looking Nevine in the eye.

"Was the whole family like that?" Nevine asked. "Like, ever since they came to America?"

"That's what I heard." Ms. Emily nodded. "I mean, I'm sure they had a few good eggs in the batch. Some of the Grimoires gave to charity, did some nice things, but I think that was pretty rare. From the talk I heard, most of them were cruel, selfish, and deceitful. There was a lot of mental illness in the family, a lot of tragedy. They had this nice big house to be miserable in." Ms. Emily sounded somehow frustrated. "But it didn't really do them any good, I suppose."

"That's why there are so many ghosts," Nevine speculated out loud. She remembered what Xanthae had told her about ghosts and tragedies and specters and evil deeds. There seemed to be a plentiful history of both in this house.

Ms. Emily laughed, a quick and harsh sound without any real pleasure. "Yes, I suppose there are, in one form or another. You'd be well advised to leave them alone."

"I can't," Nevine replied, almost pleadingly, and that was the truth of it. If Ms. Emily asked her to, she wouldn't be able to explain it, but it was the truth. She couldn't turn her back on the ghosts of Grimoire Manor.

Ms. Emily looked at Nevine very seriously for a moment, and then said, "You are a very remarkable young woman, Nevine Turner, and someday you are going to be a very remarkable leader in our society."

Nevine looked at her hands shyly, and for the first time all day, she was able to smile just a little bit.

"Give me a moment," Ms. Emily said, rising from her seat, and heading toward her bedroom. "I have something I think you might like."

A moment later, Nevine could hear Ms. Emily searching for something in her bedroom. Nevine stood up and walked over to the door to Joshua's room, which stood open a bit. Joshua was sitting on the floor, sorting a little pile of shiny rocks into smaller piles, then jumbling them up again and starting over. As Nevine watched, he did this over and over, rocking himself back and forth a little bit as he sat. He appeared to have no idea that Nevine was standing in his doorway. Every so often, his hand would go to his temple and pull at the hair that remained there around his bald spot.

"Joshua?" she said to him softly, but loud enough that he should have been able to hear her. He didn't react at all, didn't glance at her, didn't so much as pause in sorting his stones.

She carefully walked into his room, hoping not to upset him. Seeing that he still didn't acknowledge her, she knelt beside him and watched his actions for a moment. She said again, "Joshua?" As before, there was no response.

"He probably won't speak to you," Ms. Emily said from the doorway.

Nevine stood up, feeling as if she had been caught doing something she shouldn't, a feeling to which she was becoming accustomed at Grimoire Manor. "Oh, I'm sorry, Ms. Emily, you didn't say I could talk with your son."

"I didn't say you couldn't, either." Ms. Emily smiled. "Actually, it's good for him to have contact with others. He mostly ignores people, but maybe one day he'll learn to respond to someone. It's something they keep working on at his school. You may feel free to visit with Joshua whenever you wish, although I wouldn't hope that he'll be awfully friendly." Ms. Emily held out a book to Nevine. It was called *Parapsychology* by Richard S. Broughton. Nevine accepted the book and looked at it curiously.

"It's got some material in there about ESP and telekinesis and such," Ms. Emily explained, "although it also has some sections on ghosts. Since you seemed so interested, I thought you might like the book. I should warn you that it was written for professional psychologists, although I suspect that you'll be able to manage it."

"Thank you, Ms. Emily. That's very nice of you."

Ms. Emily guided Nevine back out to the living room. "You know that if you're really interested in the Grimoire family, the person you should be asking is the Provost. She knows much more about this house and its history than anyone else that I can think of."

"I don't think she likes me very much," Nevine said, wrinkling her nose a bit.

"I suspect she doesn't like very many people," Ms. Emily admitted, "but if it's information you want, that needn't be your concern. If you ask her nicely, I suspect that the Provost will be curious enough to discuss matters with you."

"Thank you again, Ms. Emily," Nevine said. "I suppose I should go now." Nevine turned at the doorway. "Ms. Emily, did you ever feel like you liked living here?"

Ms. Emily thought about it for a moment and said, "Except for when I was very young, and for a few years in college and when I was married, I have always lived here. This is where I belong, I suppose."

Ms. Emily hadn't exactly answered the question, but perhaps that was answer enough. Nevine nodded, and gripping her new book, left.

****

Nevine's friends were outside playing a game of kickball. Nevine wasn't in the mood for playing or exercise, though, so she went to her room to look over the book Ms. Emily had given her. The events in Prague were still so much on her mind that it was rather difficult to concentrate, but she did her best.

Christopher J. Ferguson

Parapsychology, it seemed from the book, was the study of all things that were supernatural from reading minds (telepathy), moving objects with your mind (telekinesis) and, of course, all manner of apparitions. The book said that such matters could be studied scientifically and that there was scientific evidence to support these phenomena. From what she read, she understood that many scientists remained skeptical, however, which seemed typical for adults.

Nevine thought of Xanthae as she skimmed the book and missed her guardian's guidance quite a bit. It was going to take a while for her to read through the book, but not enough time to get through much of it before she'd have to figure things out about the Hallway Ghost.

Nevine didn't have a chance to talk to Aurora until they were in bed, and so they whispered to each other in the darkness, while outside the familiar creaking on the floorboards told them their quarry still roamed the halls. Aurora, not surprisingly, was concerned for Nevine, and together they wondered if Nevine might end up back in Prague after she fell asleep. They tried to devise some kind of plan for what she would do if she did flip back, although it all seemed to boil down to this: try to wake up, run for it, and get at that lever if possible.

Aurora did have one thought. "I don't think the Ghoul is going to kill you while you're unconscious."

"Why do you say that?" Nevine asked, although she felt a glimmer of hope in Aurora's words.

"A couple of reasons," Aurora said, sitting up on one elbow. "I don't think he intended to harm you at all. You said that he shoved you aside. I think he was trying to kill that soldier the whole time, not you. He could have killed you very easily, but he went right past you. Maybe he didn't even mean to shove you that hard. You said he was almost kind to you several days before..."

"Yes, but he was almost human then," Nevine reminded her. Still, Aurora made some sense. It also reminded her of something that Xanthae had said. Xanthae thought that the tomb being open had been a trap, but had seemed to doubt the trap had been meant for the three of them. Why had Skounic suddenly appeared? Could the trap have been meant for him for some reason?

"The other thing is," Aurora was saying, "that if you're thinking that if you die in Prague, then you'll die here, well...we know you didn't die yet in Prague then, don't we? I mean, you're still alive here!"

"That's true," Nevine admitted. If the Ghoul had killed her in Prague while she was unconscious, she might very well already be dead in both places. Nevine wasn't at all certain how all that might work, but it seemed unlikely by now that she was going to simply keel over dead in the hallway.

"See, you have to have some optimism!" Aurora said. "I'm certain that you've got a fighting chance back in Prague!"

"You're right, Aurora, thank you," Nevine replied, feeling much better than she had all day.

"So, are you going to go talk to the Provost?" asked Aurora in the same tone she'd have used to ask, "So, are you going to stick your hand in the hungry lion's cage?"

"I'm going to have to," Nevine said. "But I want to do something first. Clarisse and Polly did a great job finding out about that cemetery. But I think I need to know which Grimoire the Hallway Ghost is before I talk to the Provost. That way, I'll know the right questions to ask."

"Let me guess." Aurora grinned. "You want to track the Hallway Ghost again and see what grave it goes to."

"That's what I was thinking."

"Well, count me in!" Aurora said bravely. "You have been the most exciting thing to happen to this school since I've been here. And let me tell you, with all the ghosts, this school is never boring."

"You're a great friend, Aurora." Nevine smiled, thinking how lucky she had been to find some good friends, if nothing else. "Tomorrow night, maybe?"

"Yeah, thinking about it will help me stay awake in class."

Nevine pulled her blanket over her face, trying to sleep. Nevine heard Aurora tossing and turning for a while. She had trouble falling asleep and was still awake after even the Hallway Ghost departed from the landing for the night. Nevine wondered, when she awoke, if she would be at Grimoire Manor, or in Prague, with the Ghoul of Vysehrad lurking over her. When she finally did sleep, her dreams, as might be expected, were not pleasant.

Chapter 13

The Luckiest Chapter

Nevine awoke, not in Prague with a ghoul looming over her, but rather in Newport, with a poorly prepared history test looming over her. First period was spent side by side with Aurora at their desks, silently sweating over their tests, while Ms. Donitz seemed to take pleasure in watching them struggle. Their mood was not helped by watching Fiona Applegate stride up to the teacher's desk, primly and confidently handing in her test as the first student to be done.

"If there's one thing these ghosts are definitely haunting," a traumatized Aurora said once they were in the hall between classes, "it's my chances of getting into college."

They waded through the rest of the morning without major incident. At lunch, they told Clarisse and Polly about their plans to track the Hallway Ghost to the cemetery.

"It's your funeral," Polly said.

"Thank you for the support, Polly," Aurora grumbled.

"It's not that hard," Clarisse said, sounding much more confident. "Even if you lose the ghost in the woods, just follow the trail along the cliff face. Try not to fall over the cliff though; that would end badly."

"The trail leads right up to the cemetery," Polly told them. "There's plenty of grass there, so you should be able to pick up the ghost's footprints, so long as there's a frost tonight."

Math and science were the two afternoon classes, and despite suffering through Ms. Speer's bad moods, these were the two classes where Nevine really shone. There was a certain pleasure she took in the order and structure of the two subjects and how these two classes informed her about the way the world really worked.

Aurora and Nevine ate dinner and studied side by side at their desks, trying not to let their escapades interfere too much with their schoolwork, although it certainly was difficult. Then, as they had done before, they remained in their daytime clothes, waiting for the Hallway Ghost to come and go. They still had their flashlight, which they decided it might be best to keep, despite feeling bad about the theft. They also put on their warm jackets, ready for a cold October night.

Predictable as always, the Hallway Ghost began patrolling the dorm landing around eleven o'clock. Nevine and Aurora whispered to each other nervously over the next two hours until the Ghost made its last round of the landing. Then, the two girls quietly left their room and started tracking the ghost.

Given the information they had from Polly and Clarisse, they were more confident they could hang back a bit from the ghost, so as not to provoke it. They knew that, unless it suddenly changed its routine, the ghost would exit through the backdoor, and make its way through the fence, up the cliff trail, and to the cemetery. It was only the last part they needed to investigate. The biggest risk for them would likely be in moving too fast and unintentionally catching up to the ghost, which they feared could cause it to become angry.

Downstairs, they were careful to make sure that Ms. Elmwood was on one of her rounds of the building. Sure that they weren't being observed, they slipped out the backdoor into the cold night. As Polly and Clarisse had promised, they easily found a track of footsteps in the frosted grass leading away from the mansion. Keeping a close eye out to be sure they weren't being followed, they passed behind the tall bushes to the damaged spot in the chain-link fence.

Bending down to pull the chain link back, Aurora commented, "I find it hard to picture a ghost getting down on its knees to crawl through a fence."

Nevine just held her hands out, palms up, helplessly.

Aurora was the first through the fence, followed by Nevine.

"You know," Aurora said as she stood back up, "other than eating with Victoria, this is the first time I've been outside of Grimoire Manor. Feels good. You know that if they catch us, they'll expel us for sure?"

"We'd better get moving then." Nevine led the way to the forest edge, following the trail of footsteps in the grass. As they expected, this led them to a trail up a small hill in the woods. The footsteps were no longer visible in the hard dirt, but Polly and Clarisse had told them just to follow the trail. Switching on their flashlight, they did exactly that.

The trail, at times, twisted dangerously close to the cliff face. At points, they could look down over the edge to the swirling ocean and the jagged rocks below.

To fall would mean a quick death. It was no wonder the school forbade the girls from exploring this far.

They didn't stop for long, though, but continued on and up, through the bare maple and oak trees, and patches of briars. At last, they emerged into a clearing. Above them, the moon beamed down, seeming bigger and brighter than it had at the mansion. Around them were graves, the final resting place of perhaps twenty members of the Grimoire family. There were ten free-standing stones Nevine considered more typical of American cemeteries. The stones were large, with names, dates, and quotations, oftentimes with statues of angels, just like in Prague. There also were four much larger crypts, spread out from each other as if the people within them didn't want to get too close. They looked almost like they had been carved out of small mounds in the ground, with earth and grass covering and growing over their tops. Their faces were stone, with heavy iron doors.

"Can you find the footprints?" Nevine asked, looking around at the grass in the clearing.

"I don't think we need the footprints...look!"

Aurora pointed over at one of the crypts. Its heavy iron door hung open, revealing inky blackness within.

Carefully, they snuck over to the crypt, looking all around for ghosts, jumping at every sound from the woods. They approached the opening of the crypt and shone the light around the door, then inside. There were two name plaques on the door, Genevieve (1841–1890) and Lyrre (1866–1896). The beam from the flashlight cut into the crypt, revealing a little room with two etched stone sarcophagi. Behind these was a little altar with a cross above it. This crypt was much smaller than the Grimoire tomb in Prague, but then again, it held only two bodies and presumably didn't have a tunnel leading to the local sewers.

"Wow," Aurora breathed, observing the dates on the plaques. "I've heard people say they'd rather die before they got old, but this Grimoire family sure was good at it!"

"I dunno," Nevine said. "Genevieve was forty-nine when she died. I think that's considered elderly."

"No, I think you have to be fifty-five before you're considered elderly."

"It doesn't really matter at the moment, does it? Which one do you think is the Hallway Ghost, Lyrre or Genevieve?" Nevine asked.

"If the ghost has been walking on frost all this time, maybe it tracked footsteps into the crypt?" Aurora suggested. They looked at each other uncertainly for a moment. The flashlight wasn't reaching through into the crypt well enough for them to search the floor near the door for footprints.

After a moment's doubt, Aurora gave Nevine a grin. "Tell my family I love them!" She ran for the door of the crypt.

"Wait," Nevine shouted after her, "what does that mean? You and I don't have families!"

"You're my family, Nevine!" Aurora shouted back, moving toward the crypt. She tried to examine it from outside for a moment and, appearing dissatisfied, stepped over the threshold of the crypt. She looked down at the floor for a moment, examining it with the flashlight. Nevine remained silent, worrying so much that she wanted to pull Aurora back out of the crypt. Aurora looked up suddenly and opened her mouth to say something.

At that moment, the door of the crypt slammed shut with an enormous bang, trapping Aurora on the inside.

"Aurora!" Nevine cried, rushing to the crypt. A harsh, cold wind whipped up in that instant, blowing leaves and dirt into Nevine's eyes. She caught her balance before the wind could knock her over, and managed to push her way to the crypt door. Gripping the latch in both hands, she pulled on it with all her might, but it didn't so much as move an inch. It was as if the door had been welded shut. After a few pulls, she gave up and pounded on the iron door. "Aurora, can you hear me in there? Are you okay?"

"Nevine, I can hear you!" Aurora's voice called back, faint, through the door. "Can you believe it? The flashlight's out again! Why does it always quit when I'm in the biggest trouble ever?"

"The door won't open. Is there a latch on the inside?"

"Who opens a crypt door from the inside?" Aurora cried back. "Let's try it together. You pull on three…two…one…" With the wind blowing her hair in her eyes, Nevine pulled desperately at the door. This time, the door did pull out just an inch, and then it wouldn't budge any further.

"What's holding it shut?" Aurora cried, her fingertips brushing against Nevine's.

"I don't know," Nevine answered desperately. "I think the door slamming shut damaged the hinges." It didn't feel as if they were working against an opposing force. Nothing was struggling to close the door again—it simply refused to budge. Nevine remembered what

Xanthae had told her about specters being capable of brief bursts of force. Had one of them, one of the long-dead Grimoires, damaged the door on purpose, and if so, to what end?

"Nevine," Aurora's voice was suddenly quieter and trembling. "I think something's moving in one of the coffins…I can hear something scratching at the lid…"

"Whaaaaat?!!" Nevine tugged at her hair in fear. "Okay, okay, stay calm."

"Sure, I'll just kick back and go over my physics lessons. Get me out of here!"

"Aurora, you're brilliant!" Physics lessons, of course. This was why you should never panic in an emergency, Nevine thought. You might be too afraid to think of a solution to the problem. "I'll be right back!" She heard Aurora scream a protest, but there was nothing she could do right there, holding Aurora's hand. She moved off quickly, through the clearing, stumbling her way through the gravestones to the forest edge. She kept away from the area of the cliff, as she wanted to be sure not to tumble off in the dark. Once she got to the forest, she searched around for a good-sized tree branch, one that was pretty solid and hadn't rotted.

She was trying to find a lever to put the tree branch in the crypt's latch and push against it. Because of Aurora's comment, she remembered a lesson Xanthae had given her on lever action. Using a lever, it was possible to exert more work using less force. Given that, as a teenage girl, she couldn't exert much force, only using a lever could make opening the door possible. The longer the lever, the more work she would be able to exert against the stubborn door, although that also would put more strain on the lever itself. She found a good solid branch, one she thought could withstand her pushing against it, and prepared to run back to the crypt.

Suddenly, she felt the now familiar feeling of the cold, draining sensation of her life's essence being pulled at by some external force. She stopped in her tracks, looking around for the source of it. All she could see were the leaves and dirt being whipped up by the sudden winds.

"Sophie?" whispered a voice in her ear.

Nevine turned sharply toward the voice, the big branch raised over her head, ready to be used as a club. There was nothing there, though, just the darkness. Confused, Nevine took two steps back into the cemetery. She wasn't sure…it was hard to be sure, but she didn't think the presence she felt was the Hallway Ghost. The Hallway Ghost carried with it the feeling of being lost, desperate. This wasn't the Attic Specter either, which had been all rage and hatred. Nevine was sure this was a third apparition, less threatening than either of the other two. If Nevine could sense an emotion from that one whispered word, it was surprise or confusion.

There was no time to ponder it, though. If the new ghost wasn't going to be a threat, Nevine didn't have time to attend to it. She rushed back to the crypt and slid the branch/lever through the latch. "Aurora, are you still okay in there?"

"Yeah," Aurora cried back, sounding very afraid. "But something's trying real hard to get out of its coffin. It's pushing hard against the lid, trying to get out. I think it's one of the bodies!"

Well, this was a trick that Xanthae apparently hadn't come across. Could ghosts bring their own dead corpses back to life, perhaps for short periods? Maybe it didn't matter much for most ghosts whose bodies might have been cremated or buried deep, but this one only had to push aside a lid. Nevine hoped the lid was too heavy; she remembered what Xanthae had said about ghosts not being very strong.

"Aurora, we have to try to push again, okay?"

"Okay, let me know when!"

"On three...two...one..." Again, they pushed with all of their might against the door, except that this time Nevine was pushing against the edge of the lever. With a harsh metallic groan, the door edged open a couple of more inches. Aurora was able to snake her arm and shoulder out of the door now and tried desperately to get the rest of her body through, but it still wasn't quite enough.

Inside the crypt, Nevine saw something bump one of the sarcophagus lids up hard, and it moved a couple of inches to the side. In a moment, whatever was in there would get out and pounce on Aurora. "One more time and I think we'll have it!"

"We better!"

"Okay, one...two...threeeee!" They pushed hard one last time, and it worked. There was a sharp bang as the top door hinge cracked out from the frame and the door came awkwardly loose. Aurora was out of the crypt like a bolt of lightning. Nevine had fallen to her knees when the door came open, but Aurora pulled her up and yanked her away from the crypt. Together, they ran as fast as they could through the cemetery, through the angry wind, past all the gravestones, out of the clearing, down the trail, next to the cliff, then back into view of Grimoire Manor. They sped across the clearing, and all but dove through the hole in the fence. Only when they got to the backdoor did they stop, panting and all out of breath, and looked behind them.

Nothing was chasing them. Even the whipping angry wind was gone here.

"Oh my goodness," Aurora said, doubling over to catch her breath. "I'm such an idiot."

"You were brilliant!" Nevine assured her. "You found out which one is the Hallway Ghost, didn't you?"

"Well," —Aurora huffed and coughed— "there was a damp footprint on the floor that gave me a clue. I think it was the skeleton trying to claw its way out of the coffin that removed all doubt, though. It's Genevieve."

"The mother," Nevine said, curious. "Thierry's mother...I think..." Genevieve had been the name under the older woman's picture they had taken from the attic.

"Lovely woman," Aurora hissed.

"Let's catch our breath for a moment before we go in." Nevine patted Aurora's back. "We still have to get past Ms. Elmwood again. I can't believe you went diving into that crypt!" It was probably Aurora diving into the crypt that had provoked the Hallway Ghost...Genevieve, but it had also given them the right name.

"I can't believe you left me all alone to go try a physics experiment," Aurora said, but she was laughing. "But it was just the thing, wasn't it?" She held her hand, palm up, to Nevine. "Girl power?"

Nevine slapped it enthusiastically. "Girl power!"

A half hour later, they were safely in their beds, exhausted but feeling more than a little pleased with themselves. For another half hour, they talked over and over again about the evening's wild exploits, quite giddy, now that the danger was over. It can probably be said that in Grimoire Manor, and perhaps all of Newport, there was not another duo of young girls who felt so powerful and yet, somehow, underneath all that adrenaline, still so alone. Nevine went to sleep with a smile on her face, but nonetheless, her arm remained closely entwined with her stuffed fox, as if this beast of the imagination could protect her from all the horrors that lingered in the night.

Chapter 14

The History of the Early Grimoires of Newport

The next morning at breakfast, Nevine and Aurora, with Polly and Clarisse in attendance, were able to thoroughly review all that occurred at the graveyard. Ultimately, they had to conclude that Polly and Clarisse's fears about being overwhelmed by multiple ghosts had not been unreasonable. The graveyard was a very dangerous place to visit.

Aurora was the one who did the most of the storytelling, and when she got to the part about being trapped in the crypt, Polly spoke up, "Hey, it couldn't have been this Genevieve ghost who slammed the door shut."

"Who's telling this story?" Aurora looked at her, flabbergasted.

"What do you mean, Polly?" Nevine asked, letting Aurora stew for a minute.

"Well," Polly thought, "you've been telling me that these ghosts don't really like to go through solid objects, right?"

"Just objects that are poor electricity conductors, like wood," Nevine answered, and fortunately Polly didn't ask how she knew that.

"Still, to get to the door, the ghost would have had to push Aurora aside, right? But she didn't feel

178

anything."

"You think it was a different ghost that slammed the door shut," Clarisse said, getting where Polly was going with this.

"Yeah," Polly said. "I think maybe this Attic Specter thing hoped to trap Aurora in the crypt, knowing the Hallway Ghost...Genevieve Grimoire would get angry and attack her."

"So the Attic Specter was trapping me and provoking the Hallway Ghost at the same time?" Aurora wondered out loud.

"That is one dysfunctional family," Clarisse observed.

Nevine wasn't listening closely, though. Something in their conversation had gotten her thinking. Xanthae had said that ghosts had difficulty passing through poor electrical conductors like wood, which is why they had to walk through the house and use wooden doors the same way as everyone else. From what Xanthae had said, Nevine got the impression that ghosts could pass through good electrical conductors, though. If that was the case, why did the ghost have to cut a hole in the chain-link fence to get through? After a moment's thought, it hit her. "Someone else has been going to the graveyard!" she exclaimed, interrupting their conversation.

"Who else would want to go up there?" Clarisse asked.

Nevine could only hold up her hands helplessly. "It's the only answer that makes sense. They must have been going up since before Polly and Clarisse went too, since the hole was already there."

"If that's the case, the hole could have been there

for years," Aurora observed. "We really don't know when or why someone might have gone up there."

Nevine sighed...it seemed like every time they found one answer, it was replaced by more questions. Around her, the others grew quiet, sensing her frustration.

At last, Aurora spoke, "What are you going to do about the Provost?"

"I guess I'll try to talk to her today after classes. I don't know if she'll talk to me, though. Without knowing why Genevieve Grimoire became a ghost, I don't know what we'd be able to do about getting rid of...or helping her. If the Provost doesn't help, then I don't really know who would."

Nevine was rather nervous about approaching the Provost, and was hoping the day might drag out a bit. Naturally, whenever you are dreading something in the future, time tends to fly by, just as eagerly anticipated events seem to take forever to arrive. As such, it was afternoon free time before Nevine even realized it. There was no point in putting off talking to the Provost until later. That would just mean worrying for longer, and she didn't know if the Provost might even leave and go some place else for the night. So, shaking a little bit, Nevine climbed the main staircase once again and knocked on the Provost's door.

"Enter," said the Provost, sounding distracted. Nevine found the old woman at her desk, with a pile of folders on one side of her. She seemed to be filling out some paperwork in the folders, and then shuffling them off to the other side of her desk. She looked up as Nevine entered. "Well, Miss Turner, this is something of a surprise. To what do I owe the honor?" There was something in her tone that was less respectful than her words seemed.

Nevine walked in and sat in the same hard chair as she had before. This time, she did it before she was invited to do so. This was obviously not lost on the Provost, who raised an eyebrow and got a sparkle of interest in her eye. The Provost said nothing, and Nevine got the sense she was like a dragon whose human prey had just proven clever enough to bother speaking with for a moment or two before eating. Somehow, a bit of boldness felt right to Nevine. It was a dangerous game, and she knew it; it would be too easy to push it too far and if she did so, she figured the Provost would quickly crush her.

"I wanted to ask you about the Grimoire family that moved here in 1888," Nevine said. "Miss Emily told me you know more about them than anyone."

If the Provost was taken in by flattery, it certainly didn't show. "I'll have to thank Ms. Emily for continually managing to send you my way. I am certainly too busy to give individual history lessons to young girls. That's what we have a history teacher for."

The Provost was losing interest again, and Nevine could sense it. She pushed her luck a bit further. "I want to know about the Hallway Ghost." The Provost looked at her like a fish that had just noticed the lure, and Nevine went a step further to seal it. "...Genevieve Grimoire."

The room seemed to grow noticeably warmer, and Nevine felt a flush come over her. She swallowed hard, hoping that her bold approach had worked, and hadn't merely earned herself more detention. The Provost ran her tongue over her old teeth, then laughed a little, softly, and put down her pen. Her voice practically purred as she said, "I've been guilty of underestimating you, Nevine Turner, something that I won't do again." This last bit sounded more like a threat than a compliment. "Very well. You have earned ten minutes of my time. What do you want to know about Genevieve Grimoire?"

"Everything you can tell me," Nevine said, and immediately knew it was too broad. "I want to know how she died. I want to know why she became the Hallway Ghost."

The Provost stood and began to pace before the window, a habit she seemed to have when she was instructing. "Genevieve married into the Grimoire family when she was very young. It was at that time a family of rising wealth. With some business dealings in Prague, the family became inordinately powerful. I assume for the moment that you know where Prague is?" The Provost stopped and looked down at Nevine.

Nevine nodded, saying nothing more.

The Provost continued, "When her husband Pierre took over the family business prospects, Genevieve became the matriarch of the family. Genevieve's own background is not well known, although it would appear to be documented well enough that Genevieve herself was given to long bouts of depression and erratic behavior. She alternated between showering her children with great affection and neglecting them entirely. She also infused into the Grimoire family a strain of mental defect that was to plague all successive generations. During the family's time in Prague, she experienced the death of a young daughter. It was a blow from which she never recovered.

"As she sank into melancholy, one of her sons degenerated into madness," the Provost continued, "and was committed to an asylum in Prague. At this point, the family record becomes disjointed and confused. Genevieve's husband Pierre disappeared from the record altogether. It is not known if he died in Prague or in America, although his grave is not at the family site here." Nor, Nevine realized, was his name on the tomb in Prague.

"Genevieve's son, Louis, took over control of the family finances. With his mother so depressed that she rarely left her bed, and his older brother committed to an asylum, he prepared to move the family to America, where business prospects were superior. His sister Lyrre appears to have been instrumental in helping the family to organize. By early 1888 or so, the family had left Prague for their voyage to America."

The Provost paused for a moment, as if to collect her thoughts. It gave Nevine a moment to think and process what she had been told. Nevine thought about her experiences in Prague. She remembered how she and Xanthae had learned that the Grimoires had left Prague six months before she had arrived there. She remembered too, Thierry's birth and death dates on his tomb. The importance of the two dates suddenly came to her. "They left Thierry behind, didn't they?"

The Provost regarded her with narrowed eyes, but said nothing. Nevine realized she was sitting there with her mouth open, stunned. She looked away from the Provost, to give herself a minute to contemplate the revelation. They had abandoned Thierry in the asylum and left him there, leaving him helpless while they pursued a better life in America. They had left him to die.

"Thierry Grimoire died in the asylum five months later," the Provost continued, her voice a bit softer. "For Genevieve, the death of her young daughter had been a crushing blow, but at the very least that had been due to the fickle hand of fate, that which God wills—"

"*Deus vult*," Nevine whispered, remembering the tomb.

"Very good, Miss Turner. When Genevieve learned of Thierry's death, she realized that it was unlike the death of her daughter. Genevieve hadn't been there when he needed her. She had selfishly turned him aside due to the imperfections he had inherited through her own blood. She was responsible, in many ways, for Thierry's death. It was the most unforgivable of crimes. She survived for perhaps a year and a half longer in the deepest of depressions before finally, one night, she walked to the cliffs next to Grimoire Manor and hurled herself onto the rocks below. Hers was the first tragic Grimoire death in America. The first, I am sad to say, of many."

Nevine felt very sad, sad for Genevieve, sad for Thierry, and she knew that it must have shown on her face. The Provost watched her as one might watch a most interesting specimen. At last, Nevine looked up and asked, "Why does she haunt Grimoire Manor? Why doesn't she go back to Prague, where Thierry died?"

The Provost made an uncertain gesture with her wrinkled lips. "My guess is that she can't. Perhaps she haunts Grimoire Manor because she is anchored to the misery she knows here."

"Do you think that Thierry haunted her to death?" Nevine asked.

"No." The Provost shook her head. "I think that Genevieve haunted herself to death."

"So she's trapped here because she can't be forgiven?"

The Provost took her seat in her chair and folded her hands before her face. "Although some people think of Hell as a place of fire and pain where the physical body is tortured, many priests today think that Hell is simply being kept isolated from God. Hell is thought of as a spiritual loneliness. If that is the case, then I suspect Genevieve Grimoire has found that she did not need to travel far at all to find Hell."

"Do you think that it's possible to do anything for her?" Nevine asked hesitantly.

The Provost looked at her critically. "It's always dangerous to tinker too much with the natural ecology of things. There's no need to worry terribly about Genevieve Grimoire. She is entirely harmless, so long as you leave her be. Besides, an intelligent young woman such as yourself should be concentrating on your studies, rather than worrying so much about the failings of a woman long dead."

Nevine didn't have anything to say in reply. What the Provost said made some sense, of course. She knew as well as anyone that she was out of her league in taking on the Ghosts of Grimoire Manor. Yet, she was somehow driven to keep trying, as if in doing this, she had found her purpose in life. She couldn't turn her back on Genevieve Grimoire, no matter what the woman might have once done to her son. Nevine couldn't accept that some wrongs could not be undone.

The Provost was studying her, and finally let her gaze drop as if disappointed. "Of course, no one takes my good advice; I'm just an old woman. I trust that I've told you all that you wanted to hear?"

"Yes," Nevine said, sliding off the chair as she sensed she was being dismissed. At the door, she turned back to the Provost. "I don't suppose that you know anything about the specter who haunts the attic?" She had lost her boldness and the likelihood she could convince the Provost to tell her more was low and she knew it.

The Provost had already returned to her work and didn't look up. "You've already used up more of my time than I like to give to most students. Now, if I were you, Miss Turner, I'd get going before I give you detention just because I can."

Nevine closed the door behind her quietly and ran off to join her friends. She felt sorry for the Hallway Ghost...Genevieve Grimoire. It sounded as if her life had been so unhappy. Abandoning her son had been a terrible thing to do, although it had ultimately killed her as well. Nevine wanted to think there could be some way of undoing the misery they had both experienced.

That night, she thought about Genevieve Grimoire for a long time, staring out her window while Genevieve's ghost walked the halls outside their room.

"You're thinking about her, aren't you?" Aurora whispered from across the room.

Nevine turned over in her bed and nodded.

"Do you think we'll be able to help her?"

"I don't know," Nevine said. "I don't know how to fix this. It's not like in the movies where they just say a few prayers and sprinkle holy water around and the ghosts go away."

"I think in the movies, the ghost usually ends up

burning the house down." Aurora frowned. "I hope that's not an option here. I don't think this place is up on its fire codes."

"If I don't get turned into a ghoul in Prague, maybe I'll be able to ask Xanthae what she thinks I should do."

"It really is a sad story in a lot of ways, isn't it?" Aurora whispered. "I'm not sure if it makes me more or less frightened of them to know how miserable the ghosts are."

"More frightened," Nevine whispered back. "So many years of misery must have made them insane. I think we're lucky that the ghosts seem not to notice us most of the time. I think they must hate us when they see us."

Aurora looked at her across the dark room and pulled the blankets up to her eyes. Outside, a creaking floorboard announced that Genevieve Grimoire was pacing across again in her lonely vigil. Nevine turned back over to watch the night from her window. She clutched her stuffed fox to her chest and willed her eyes to close. At last, after Genevieve left the landing for the night, they did, and Nevine finally slept.

****

The first thing she noticed when she awoke was the faint smell of burning oil. The second thing she noticed was the splitting pain in her head. She was distantly aware that she was having some trouble thinking straight, as if pushing sleep away was particularly difficult this morning.

It wasn't morning at all, of course, she began to realize as she pushed her face away from the cold stone of the Grimoire family tomb in Prague. Her arms were so weak that it was difficult for them to support her weight. Instead, she rolled onto her back and reached up to her forehead, and felt a painful and bloody lump there.

Somewhere through the fog of her awareness, she could hear Xanthae calling out her name, but it seemed so distant. She rolled over to the side to try to get a better sense of her surroundings. She found herself staring at Skounic's face. She only recognized him from his clothes, dirty now, but still in the white Austrian uniform. His face consisted of dry, crumbled skin, and his eyes were vacant, dark sockets. His pistol had skittered away when he had fallen, and his jaw hung open as if in an endless scream.

Nevine's mouth opened in shock, but she didn't have the energy to scream. Her eyes scanned around the room, although this hurt her head. The burning torches still cast their light around, but aside from herself and Skounic, there seemed to be no one else. The Ghoul of Vysehrad was gone.

Again, from the distance, she heard Xanthae's voice calling her name.

She forced herself up onto one arm, trying to get herself sorted out. She opened her mouth to shout, "Xanthae," but it came out as a strained and hoarse cough.

"Nevine, is that you?" Xanthae called again. "Answer me, please!"

Nevine rubbed her forehead and took a deep breath to prepare to shout again. She didn't have a chance, however. She caught a flicker of movement out of the corner of her eye. Looking down at Skounic, she seemed to see his body twitch. A moment later, his skull shifted so that his black eye sockets stared directly at her. His jaw opened a bit further, and his lungs released their last breath in a long, hungry sigh.

Chapter 15

Undeath of a Soldier

Nevine struggled to her knees, scrambling to put distance between herself and Skounic. The injury to her head was still getting the better of her, and she felt weak and wobbly. Distantly, she wondered if this was what a concussion felt like. Either way, she didn't feel good at all—trying to move so quickly made her feel very nauseous. Adrenaline kicked in, however, which helped. She had to force her body to move or Skounic would kill her and turn her body into yet another ghoul. How ironic it would have been for her to have been spared by Thierry Grimoire only to be killed immediately upon returning to Prague by Skounic.

She was able to put a few feet of distance between herself and Skounic, and using one of the pillars, she managed to pull herself to her feet. This was too much for her body to bear, and she had to hug the pillar to keep from falling over. Another wave of nausea washed over her, and she doubled over, vomiting painfully onto the floor of the tomb.

Behind her, the Skounic ghoul struggled to its knees, the once immaculate uniform now ruined by dirt and grime. His skeletal face watched Nevine hungrily, the jaw clicking open and shut, open and shut rhythmically. She wondered if he might have been trying to say something, but there was no sound other than his teeth clicking. Suddenly, he lurched out and his skeletal fingers grasped at the hem of her dress. She cried out and pulled away from him, and the dress tugged out of his fingers. She was fortunate that, like her, he too was still weak, although he seemed to be gaining strength faster than she was.

Nevine wished more than anything that Xanthae was here to help her, but of course, Xanthae and Petyr were still trapped behind the portcullis. Taking a few unsteady steps away from Skounic again, Nevine raced through her options. On one hand, she could try running down the corridor to Xanthae and Petyr, although she was unsure what good that could do. She would herself be between Petyr and the ghoul, and Petyr wouldn't effectively be able to use the flamethrower to save her. The only real option was to try to get to the lever. She had been very sure that it was in the sarcophagus that held the little girl. Now, with only seconds to decide, she was no longer certain. It had seemed a reasonable guess, but what if she were wrong? If she went searching inside that sarcophagus, she would be trapped and Skounic would get her for sure. Even if she released the lever, would Xanthae and Petyr be able to get up the hall to her in time?

There really was no other option, however. Skounic was blocking the only exit and now rising to his feet, becoming ever steadier in his ghoulish state. Nevine was going to have to believe in her instinct about the lever. Summoning what energy she had remaining, she darted for the sarcophagus and began pulling herself up and inside it. The lid was still halfway on the casket, giving Nevine a bit of protection on the inside. The stone was still warm to the touch, having recently been burned by the flamethrower, but it was no longer dangerously hot. The inside was black and sooty, and smelled strongly of kerosene and burned bones, and was not pleasant in the least. The remains of the little girl were still there, although these now consisted mainly of burned and shattered bone fragments, hardly recognizable as human any longer. Nevine didn't like having to do what she was about to do, but there was no other choice.

Holding her breath, Nevine hoisted herself over the lid of the crypt and dropped down inside it, lying on her stomach. She could feel the bone bits from the little girl everywhere, and this very nearly made her sick again. Toward the head of the sarcophagus, the part that had been easily visible, Nevine had not seen a lever. It either had to be at the foot of the coffin, or Nevine was wrong and she would be doomed. She crawled in further under the lid of the sarcophagus and began feeling around with her hands.

Outside the sarcophagus, she heard the Skounic ghoul moving now. The click-clack of his military shoes against the stone was obviously moving after her, coming for the sarcophagus. After a moment, a shadow fell across what little light got under the sarcophagus lid and she knew that he now had her trapped inside.

Desperately, with her heart pounding, she searched with her hands in the dark for the lever she knew had to be there. It just had to be there—she simply couldn't believe that she was meant to die like this and have her body turned into a horrible monster. At last, at the very foot of the sarcophagus, her hands found a little lever, and desperately pulled at it. It wouldn't move down any further than it already was, so she pulled it upward, hoping that was the right thing to do. It moved, and she listened in the distance for the sound of the gate rising, but she couldn't be sure one way or another if she had been successful.

Skounic's hands were on her now, his bony fingers gripping her legs. The feeling of them, so stiff and dry, scratching her exposed legs, repulsed her. She kicked and kicked and screamed with all the breath left in her lungs. She succeeded in loosening his grasp at first, but he managed to get hold of her legs and pulled her halfway out of the sarcophagus. He now bent down over the sarcophagus, the remains of his face getting ever closer to her own, and he sighed again. This time, the contents of his lungs reached her face, and she could smell the horrible odor of death and decay.

Acting almost on instinct, she reached into her coat and pulled out one of the flares she had kept with her. As Skounic leaned in further, she pulled the cap on the flare, and it burned to life with its red sparkling flame. Skounic immediately released his grip and staggered back a few steps, startled and repulsed by the light. Burning bits of magnesium fell on Nevine's face and hands, thankful they did not set her hair on fire.

The flare had worked as well as she could have hoped. She knew, however, from the female ghoul who had almost gotten Petyr, that the ghouls could be cunning and would try to get past the flares if they could. Still, she was able to clamber out of the sarcophagus. As she did so, Skounic watched her hungrily, never venturing more than a few feet from the reach of the flare. He had positioned himself between her and the exit, so there was still no way for her to flee.

At that moment, Xanthae emerged from the tunnel to the north, her pistol held ready. Petyr was just behind her, goggles over his face, flamethrower equipped. Skounic turned toward them, and his jaw dropped open, sighing at them—perhaps the only sign of frustration and anger he could manage.

Xanthae steadied her pistol and fired a shot into Skounic's chest. He went stumbling back, his feet and hands skittering about to maintain his standing position. Xanthae stepped forward, moving between Skounic and Nevine. She fired again, and Skounic continued to be pushed back. The bullets were not harming the ghoul, but he was being forced back against the far wall of the crypt, giving Nevine an opening to get to the exit, and Petyr a clear shot with the flamethrower.

Xanthae stepped forward again, firing her pistol into Skounic a third time. She glanced quickly at Nevine, her expression grim. "Go, run while you can!" she ordered, her voice tolerating no dissent.

Nevine moved as ordered, summoning what little fuel she had left to move for the stairs up to some fresh air. Xanthae pulled back away from the ghoul, to follow closely behind Nevine, and guard her retreat. Into this opening left by Xanthae stepped Petyr who, without a word, poured flaming kerosene onto Skounic.

Nevine was up and out then, back into the cold December night. Her lungs rejoiced at the fresh, scentless air. The rest of her body was done with any exertion, however; her head felt like it was splitting open, her stomach was tied in knots, and her limbs felt as if her bones had turned to butter. She held out one of her arms to steady herself on the iron fence that surrounded the outer crypts. Her hand missed the fence and she began to tumble, no longer having the power to stop herself. Before she hit the ground, Xanthae's arms were around her, preventing her from falling.

Dimly, she was aware of being in Xanthae's embrace, with the snow still falling lightly on her face. Xanthae was speaking; her voice soft and soothing, but Nevine couldn't understand what she was saying. It didn't matter, though; all that mattered was that the last thing Nevine knew before her eyes closed again was the comforting sound of her guardian's voice.

****

She slept fitfully that night and recovered into the next day. Xanthae attended to her very carefully, washing her wound, bringing her food, spending hours speaking with her when she was awake, trying to make Nevine as comfortable as possible. As evening the next day began to approach, Nevine was feeling considerably better and her headache was largely gone.

As the sun was setting, and Nevine truly beginning to perk up, Xanthae came to speak with her, bringing a little plate of sliced apples with her. "You are feeling better?"

"Much better," Nevine said, delighted by the apples. It had taken almost twenty-four hours, but she was feeling quite herself again.

"I'm glad to hear it," Xanthae said, sitting on the edge of Nevine's bed. "Now that you're feeling well, we should probably talk about things and decide what we're going to do next."

Nevine popped an apple slice in her mouth and nodded. "You've figured some things out, haven't you?" she asked through a mouth full of apple bits.

Xanthae nodded. "I think so, but I'd like to see what your opinion is as well."

Nevine was quiet for a moment, thinking. In truth, she had been thinking of the incidents in the Grimoire crypt all day. Even in her dreams, the Skounic ghoul had returned, his claws grasping her legs, his deathly breath sighing into her face. She thought that she might have figured a few things out too, although she was new at this and didn't entirely trust her instincts. Tentatively, she asked, "The trap was for Skounic, wasn't it?"

Xanthae nodded. "Yes, I suspect so very much. I regret to say that I think I may be partially responsible for that as well."

"Why do you say that?"

Xanthae frowned. "At the masquerade ball, I told Skounic about the crypt. As I had mentioned to you, I thought that he and Novak might have been more successful in tracking down information than we were, and I didn't care if we forfeited the mayoress' bounty in order to catch the ghoul. I trust that you told no one at the ball about the crypt yourself?"

Nevine shook her head. She had figured it best to keep quiet about it.

Xanthae watched Nevine carefully. Her eyes seemed particularly bright and sparkling tonight, a flame from a candle in Nevine's room flickering in their pupils. "You will, by now, have realized who is responsible for Thierry Grimoire's transformation into the ghoul?"

Nevine thought for a moment. "I want to think that it's Dr. Viliček, because we know he's in the Society for Metaphysical Research. But I never told him anything about the crypt." Xanthae said nothing, letting Nevine think it out for herself. Nevine didn't really like the only other conclusion she could reach. "It had to be Novak then, didn't it? I was wondering why he wasn't with Skounic at the crypt. I didn't want to think that because Novak seemed like such a nice man."

Xanthae nodded. "I think that you, Petyr, and I are lucky that Skounic wanted the mayoress' bounty still. When I told him about the crypt, he must have then told Novak, but taken the credit for the discovery himself. Otherwise, Novak would have sent the Ghoul of Vysehrad after us. Novak must have known that Skounic was going to investigate the tomb and realized Skounic was getting too close to uncovering his own involvement in the Ghoul of Vysehrad. It's likely Novak was a member of the Society of Metaphysical Research like Dr. Viliček, although I don't think that Novak's research with the Vysehrad Ghoul was sanctioned by the Society. Still, that's likely where he learned the dark invocations necessary to raise the ghoul from the dead."

"So Novak was trying to learn how to resurrect someone, and Thierry Grimoire was just a research subject?"

Xanthae nodded. "It seems likely. Thierry Grimoire had been abandoned by his family, and the Grimoire family tomb must have made an ideal location for the initial research. Novak probably got information on the tomb itself from the Society. I have my suspicions that some members of the Grimoire family may once have been members of the Society themselves. Not Thierry, though, I suspect. I think that he is himself, a victim in these events."

Nevine thought a little more. "Novak mentioned that he had a son who was killed in the army. I wonder if he was going to try to resurrect his son? Only the Vysehrad Ghoul never really worked well, he kept decaying…"

"…and needing regular infusions of new life energy," Xanthae finished for her. "Thierry Grimoire was a failed experiment, but one that must have looked tantalizingly promising to someone as desperate for success as Novak was. He refused to give up on his creation, despite the havoc that it wreaked. Whether he could control the ghoul's regular feedings, I don't know…but I am sure that he caused the ghoul to target Skounic, and so we can not doubt Novak is capable of murder."

"It's so sad, really," Nevine said, looking down. "I wonder why Thierry Grimoire was kind to me that day we saw him in the cemetery. And why didn't he kill me as well as Skounic?"

"Well, the ghoul did try to kill you the first day you arrived in the city. What was different about you those later two days from the first day that you arrived in Prague?" Xanthae asked with a little gleam in her eye as though trying to see if Nevine could guess the answer.

Nevine thought and thought and thought for some minutes as her fingers fidgeted with the little diamond that hung on the chain around her neck. Of course, she realized, this was what had changed about her. "The mayoress' necklace. She gave that to me because she knew it would protect me. I wonder why the necklace was so special?"

"I would guess that it belonged to Thierry's

Grimoire's younger sister, Sophie, in whose sarcophagus the lever had been located. In seeing the necklace, he must have thought you were Sophie. He must have loved her deeply for that level of affection to have survived his transformation into undeath."

"So the mayoress saved my life in a way." Nevine found that amazing somehow. "Do you think that she knows about me? That I'm not from this time…"

"It's hard to know what that one knows or suspects. She does seem to have taken an interest in you at minimum." Xanthae's expression darkened. "I'd warn you not to put too much trust into one act of kindness. I've always suspected the mayoress of involvement with the Society for Metaphysical Research. We must wonder how this device of your salvation came to be in her possession in the first place."

"When Novak raised Thierry Grimoire from the dead, he gained some control over him in his ghoul state," Nevine said. "But with the necklace on, I can convince him not to hurt us, can't I? I can break Novak's control over Thierry."

"That is quite possible," Xanthae said with a smile. "Although I would rather keep you here in safety, it may be important that you join Petyr and me as we destroy the ghoul for good."

"I want to help!" Nevine said, too loudly, and her head ached a little bit. "There's no way that I am going to learn to become a ghost hunter without doing it."

"You are very brave," Xanthae said, meeting Nevine's gaze similar to a mother's love. "Very well. I suspect that we were wrong all along about the Ghoul staying in the tomb. Seeing him at the cemetery that one day must have just been chance…he may have been paying his respects to his sister in his own fashion. I believe he has been staying at a house Novak owns in the city."

Nevine felt a burst of both nervousness and excitement. "When do we go confront them?" she asked.

Xanthae gave Nevine a critical look, as though assessing her health. "It would be best to go sooner. I suspect the Society for Metaphysical Research will presently guess that Novak has been conducting research on the ghoul without their sanction. They'll want to keep the ghoul for their own research. Once Dr. Viliček and the SMR have gotten control of the ghoul, tracking and destroying it will be much more difficult."

"I can go tonight!" Nevine volunteered. In truth, she felt afraid of the prospect of confronting Novak and wondered whether she'd be able to break the man's control over the Ghoul of Vysehrad. She knew this was important, though, and if risking her own life could potentially save others, what choice did she really have?

Xanthae's critical appraisal of Nevine's health continued for a moment until she seemed satisfied. "It's very important that you do anything I say when we go to Novak's home. I doubt he'll be expecting us, but he might be prepared for anything. This will certainly be very dangerous. Are you sure that you're ready?"

"I am ready," Nevine assured her, patting her hand. "I won't let you down."

"I'm certain you won't." Xanthae smiled.

Chapter 16

Fire and Brimstone

As they had done the night before, the three of them prepared for a difficult night. Flares, Xanthae's pistol, oil of vitriol, and Petyr's flamethrower: their tool kit was, by now, becoming quite familiar. As they left the observatory, night had fallen and the air was becoming cold and so, as before, they rented a carriage into the city. The carriage driver gave them an odd look but asked no questions.

Novak's home was in the northeast part of the city, and it proved to be a somewhat larger home than Nevine expected. It was nothing comparable to Grimoire Manor, but it was several stories tall and set on a small parcel of land that separated it a bit from the surrounding buildings. Despite the size of the house, it did not look particularly nice or elegant, and looking around at the area in general, Nevine got the impression this area might once have been well-to-do, but had since fallen out of favor. The homes were generally large but neglected, and some were abandoned altogether.

Seeing the house from inside the carriage, Xanthae expressed that its separation from the nearby homes was a benefit. "These homes are all built mainly from wood," she explained, "which means that the risk of using the flamethrower is considerable. At least the houses are not so close that a fire spreading is likely. Petyr, try to be as careful with your aim as possible. However, we must all be aware that once the house begins to catch fire, which ultimately is likely, we must make escape our first priority. It will take only minutes for that house to be engulfed in flame."

With that warning in their minds, they stepped out of the carriage and dismissed the driver. They would have to try their luck at finding another carriage on the way home. Slowly, and with a sense of dread, they crossed the street to the home of the soldier Novak and the Ghoul of Vysehrad that he had created. The house appeared mainly to be dark, although a few windows showed the soft glow of candle or lantern light.

As they stepped up to the heavy front door, they looked at each other uncertainly for a moment. "Do you think we should knock?" Nevine asked, although she knew that it sounded silly.

Petyr, with the flamethrower tanks on his back, goggles on his face, and signature top hat, was just lighting up the methane burners with a match. "I don't suspect I'm the sort of fellow someone would open a door for at the moment."

Xanthae reached into her cloak and produced the oil of vitriol and a thin glass pipette. "Normally it is rude to enter someone's house without first knocking, but I think that we'll likely need to make an exception this time." She used the pipette to carefully draw out the oil of vitriol and release it into the lock. The acid did not harm the glass pipette but immediately produced vapor, once introduced into the lock. After a few moments, the lock was disabled. The door apparently was not latched or barred, and swung open at Xanthae's touch.

The air within the house was slightly warmer than the outside air and smelled of harsh chemicals. Just inside the front door, a wooden set of stairs led up toward the second floor. The bottom floor was entirely dark, but a little glow came from up the stairs. On the walls of the entryway were a few portraits; a painting of a younger Novak and a woman who must have been his wife; as well as a black-and-white photograph of a young man in an Austrian military uniform. Even in the entryway, they could see that the house's interior was neglected. There were cobwebs in the corners, and the furniture looked to be in disarray.

Closing the front door behind them, they looked around a little in the entrance rooms, but it seemed clear their quarry was not on the bottom floor. They stuck together very carefully, Nevine with a flare ready, Xanthae with her pistol aimed in front of them. Although they didn't speak, they realized it was going to be difficult to sneak up on their prey, as their feet set floorboards creaking, and their movements were always announced by the steady hiss of the flamethrower's methane burners.

Xanthae motioned them upstairs and carefully they began climbing with Petyr in the lead and Xanthae just behind him. The stairway twisted up toward the third floor. The light from the second floor was coming from a sitting room off of the main hall in which a fire was slowly cackling. The fire did little to warm much more than the immediate room and Nevine could see her breath hang in the air as she breathed. The sitting room was filled with shelves of books and several plush chairs, but was otherwise empty. If nothing else, however, the fire was a good indication that Novak was in the home someplace.

Aside from the sitting room, the second floor was dark and quiet like the first, and their cursory search of the rooms revealed nothing out of the ordinary. They were aware of the danger this search posed. Indeed, either Novak or Thierry Grimoire might have been hiding in the many dark corners of the house, and it would have proven difficult to spot them until they attacked. They could only hope that Novak had not been anticipating their arrival.

Up the next staircase they went, to yet another landing. By the light of the methane burners, they could see the stairway ended in a corridor that went left and right, and they chose to start their search to the left. This led them to a large bedroom in the corner of the house, which appeared to be empty of people, and another corridor. Another soft glow came from this hallway, and carefully they crossed through it, seeing it crossed over yet a third hallway that led through the center of the house, parallel with the landing.

As they turned the corner, they could see that this corridor ascended perhaps twenty feet until it came to the back of the house. There were two doorways off the corridor, one halfway down to the left, and one down to the right. The corridor itself ended in a little alcove with a desk and candelabra, from which the glow was emanating. The same symbol etched into the Grimoire family tomb, the Black Sun, had been painted above the desk. At the desk sat the hunched-over figure of Novak, in his uniform pants and shirt, his back to them as he wrote slowly and meticulously in a large book. To his right side on the desk sat a revolver, the flickering of the candle lights glimmering on its steel surface.

Quietly, with Xanthae in the lead, they moved closer to Novak until they were halfway down the corridor next to the door on the left. Without turning to face them, Novak set his pen down, and his hand edged toward the revolver.

"Don't," Xanthae said, the single word filled with menace, her pistol aimed at his back.

"Dr. Halruaa," he said, his voice calm but somehow sad. "What a pleasant surprise. I had been expecting Dr. Viliček, but I see that you have pieced things together first. I might be allowed to stand at least, so I might face you?"

"Slowly," Xanthae warned.

Novak stood carefully, with his hands raised. In the light of the candelabra, he looked old and tired. His expression was sorrowful and resigned, and it was the latter part that made Nevine worry. "I see you have brought your clever pupils with you. I knew that with Skounic's death, I would have little time left to try to understand where my experiment had failed. I assume you know what I have done and why?"

"I am trying to understand why you would think of doing such a thing. Why have you done this to Thierry Grimoire, who never did harm to you?" Xanthae asked.

Novak looked down. "He had been abandoned by his family. I thought that in making him the trial subject of my experiment, I would be showing him much more favor than his own family had done. I would have taken care of him...I have tried to take care of him. I did not mean to make a monster out of him."

"What did you think that you would do?" Xanthae

demanded.

"The golden sun gives life to everything on earth," Novak tried to explain. "I thought that the Black Sun could bring life back to the dead. Still, somehow, I think it is possible, only that I have the invocations wrong…"

Xanthae seemed speechless in the face of his persistence. In the moment of silence, Nevine asked, "You wanted your son back, didn't you?"

Novak nodded. "It was difficult enough for me when my wife died. Losing my own child, though…that was too much to bear. He hadn't wanted to join the army—he did it because it was my wish and it made me proud. He died in order to please me, and I couldn't let that be. I knew the Society for Metaphysical Research did work on the dead, and so I joined with them, and learned their secrets."

"If Dr. Viliček captures the ghoul," Xanthae hissed angrily, "you will have done such great harm to the people of Prague as you could never imagine." She shook her head, calming herself. "Do the right thing, Novak. Help us destroy what you have created. Let the spirit of Thierry Grimoire rest."

Novak looked at her sadly. "I'm afraid there's to be no redemption for me, Dr. Halruaa. There can be no return from the road that I've chosen."

At that moment, Petyr called out in alarm. Nevine and Xanthae both turned to see that Thierry Grimoire, back in his human visage and wearing a long black cloak, had stepped silently into the hallway behind them. He might have been hiding in the bedroom, or one of the floors below, but he had eluded their search. Now they were trapped between him and Novak.

Thierry Grimoire watched the three of them with an emotionless expression, as if he wasn't sure about what to think of these visitors.

Petyr pulled the flamethrower around, bringing it to bear on Thierry Grimoire, but Thierry's ghoulish reflexes were not lost in his revitalized form. He gripped the nozzle of the flamethrower and twisted it upward just as Petyr released a column of burning kerosene. The flaming liquid spread along one corner of the ceiling and the far wall, and began burning the wood of the house. The acrid smell of smoke and burning kerosene immediately filled the hall. Thierry Grimoire stepped closer to Petyr, attempting to grapple him.

Seeing this, Nevine shouted out, "No, Thierry!" and the Ghoul turned and looked at her as she shouted this, his expression softening ever so slightly. He released his grip on Petyr and turned as if to run.

Nevine did not see what happened to them next, for a deafening boom rang out in the hall, and Nevine turned to see a red streak cut across Xanthae's right shoulder. In the moment's confusion, Novak had retrieved his revolver and had just missed blowing Xanthae's head off. Xanthae had turned to see it coming and had twisted just enough to get hit in the shoulder instead. She was able to raise her pistol and fire back, and Nevine saw Novak stumble, colliding clumsily against the desk, before raising his revolver to fire at them again.

Thinking quickly, Nevine tried the knob on the door to their left and found it open. She pushed the door open and pulled Xanthae into the dark room after her, just as Novak's second shot whizzed through the space where Xanthae had just been standing. Xanthae and Nevine went tumbling into the dark room, away from the melee outside.

Nevine was up and on her feet quickly, pulling Xanthae back up to a standing position. "You were hit!" she cried. "Are you all right?"

Xanthae steadied herself against the wall. "I think it's just, as they say, a flesh wound, but I must admit it hurts quite a bit! Still, I can use my hand. What about you? Are you all right?"

"I'm fine, Dr. Halruaa. Petyr's in danger, though!"

"The house is on fire, as well. We must find Petyr and get out at once." The room they were in had no exit, save for the door they had come in through, and so Xanthae carefully approached the opening, with her pistol ready. The main hallway proved to be empty. However, Petyr, Novak, and Thierry Grimoire were all gone. Novak looked to have taken the book he had been writing in and escaped through the furthest door. Down the hall where they had entered, the entire wall and ceiling were now in flames and radiated heat like a furnace. The fire was spreading quickly too, particularly up and over the ceiling, where a thick layer of black smoke was accumulating.

"Keep your head down," Xanthae shouted. "The cleanest air will be toward the floor level."

It would be no more than a minute before the entire hallway was in flames. They quickly began moving out into the hall, past the desk. The doorway here was open, and it led down through another hallway. At the end was another open door and a dark room beyond. Xanthae paused for a moment in case Novak waited in ambush. There were no shots. It seemed Novak must have been most intent on his own escape. Of Petyr and the Ghoul, there was still no sign.

With the fire right behind them, they moved down through the hallway, hoping this would prove to be a viable exit. Light from the fire kept the hall reasonably lit. As they passed halfway through the hall, there was an audible click, and suddenly the floor fell out from beneath them. A trapdoor opened under their weight, revealing a considerable drop, at least thirty feet, straight down into the basement. Feeling a rush of panic, Nevine spun and lashed out behind her with her hands. She managed to grab onto the edge of the floor and momentarily keep herself from falling. She was in a most desperate predicament, however, and knew it well. Her feet were dangling over a dangerous fall, and even if she could pull herself up, which she doubted, she would be trapped on the side of the hallway with the fire.

Xanthae had managed to grasp hold of the opposite edge of the trap. "Nevine, hold on!" she shouted, her voice full of alarm. She tried to reach out for Nevine with one arm, but there was too much distance between them, and with one shoulder wounded, she could barely hold on herself.

Suddenly, through the smoke, Petyr emerged in the room across from the trap. His goggles still on, and flamethrower still ready, he rushed to Xanthae, put his hands under her shoulders, and helped her up to safety. With Xanthae safe for now, he called out, "Hold on for just a moment. I'm going to find something to throw to you…" He went desperately around the far room, but Nevine could tell from his frantic search he wasn't finding anything remotely useful as a rope.

Xanthae was still trying to reach out to her from across the gap, tears running tracks in her soot-stained face, calling out Nevine's name again and again and begging her to hold on. Nevine somehow found this was the worst thing; that she was somehow guilty for making her guardian worry about her so much. This was worse than fearing for her own life and the knowledge that she was seconds from death.

Looking down, Nevine could see only darkness. The walls of the chute that led down to her death flickered a bit in the fire from the hallway, but the pit itself seemed almost to have no end. The light from the flames grew dim after a moment and Nevine looked up to find that Thierry Grimoire stood above her over the trap, silhouetted by the roaring flames behind him. He looked down at her, his expression almost confused, before he knelt. and reached out with one hand, grabbing her wrist. How cold his touch was, how immensely cold. It was as if her own heat were being stolen from her and sucked into Thierry's body. He was strong, though, and he lifted her, pulling her up into the hallway beside him.

"Nevine!" Xanthae called, and Nevine turned to see Xanthae and Petyr both at the edge of the room, across from the trap, watching as the Ghoul pulled her up. They both looked uncertain as to what to do. Petyr had his flamethrower ready, but there was no way he could harm Thierry Grimoire without also burning Nevine. Yet, safe though she might be from the pit trap, Nevine was still on the wrong side of the pit, about to be engulfed with Thierry Grimoire, by waves of flame.

Thierry Grimoire regarded her with sad, bloodshot eyes. His jaw opened, and he sighed his deathly sigh.

This time, however, he managed a single word and it was unmistakable, "Sophie..."

Nevine knew then that the third apparition at the Grimoire cemetery in Newport had been Thierry Grimoire. She wondered somehow if Thierry's spirit had come back with her as she had flipped between Prague and Newport, or if his spirit had lingered in Grimoire Manor for so many years until recognizing her from this past. Either way, she knew Xanthae was wrong about one thing...destroying the Ghoul of Vysehrad was not going to be enough to give Thierry Grimoire's soul rest. That was going to require something more.

Ignoring the roaring flames for a moment, she took Thierry's hand in her own. It was cold, colder even than holding a piece of ice, but she forced herself to hold it. "Genevieve...our mother..." It felt bad to lie to him about being his sister, but she had no other options. "What she did to you was wrong. But it has destroyed her, and she knows only the deepest sorrow for what she has done. Neither she nor you will ever be able to rest until you forgive her for what she did. Do you understand me?"

She hoped he could understand English because she didn't know any French and not enough Czech to say that much. There was no time for Xanthae to try to translate. The rest of the Grimoire family must have spoken English to move to America, so she hoped he did too. Thierry Grimoire regarded her for a moment, sadness etched on his face. At last, he nodded, a barely perceptible movement of his head. With that, he gripped her by the wrist once more and extended her out over the open pit, holding onto the wall with one hand. He stretched as far as he could, trying to bring her within reach of Xanthae and Petyr.

Her two friends were both up and reaching out for her. With her wounded shoulder, Xanthae could barely keep steady, but Petyr's grip was strong and sure, and his hands met hers. He pulled her out of the Ghoul's grip into Xanthae's waiting arms.

Thierry Grimoire remained standing at the edge of the pit, with the roaring flames just behind him now. The three of them watched him for a second, expecting him to run, even jump down the pit to save himself, but he did nothing. Tentatively, Petyr raised the flamethrower in Thierry's direction. Thierry Grimoire did nothing to save himself but merely closed his eyes.

Xanthae shielded Nevine's eyes as well, an instinctive motherly gesture, and then somehow thought better of it and dropped her hand. If Nevine was going to become a ghost hunter, she was going to need to learn to deal with some most horrible things. With Xanthae holding her tightly, Nevine watched as Petyr unleashed a cone of burning kerosene onto the Ghoul, who merely stood there and accepted it. A second later, he crumpled to the floor and was dead.

"We've got to go," Xanthae said, pulling Nevine up. They followed Petyr back to the stairway and then quickly down and out. Finally, they emerged into the cold but clear air, each of them covered with soot, sweat, and, in Xanthae's case, blood. The roof of the house was, by now, engulfed in flame, and it was clear that in another minute or two, they would have had no hope of escape.

They ran through the little yard and to the street and stopped there only because they found a carriage waiting. Beside the carriage was Dr. Viliček and a tall blond man who held a pistol ready. Novak was kneeling at Dr. Viliček's feet. Like the three of them, Novak was covered in soot, and in obvious pain, bleeding from the gunshot wound.

"Well, Ms. Turner," Dr. Viliček said pleasantly as if they were meeting at an afternoon luncheon, "Dr. Halruaa, and your esteemed student, Mr. Weiss. I am pleased to see that you weren't consumed in that most unfortunate conflagration." Dr. Viliček motioned up at the emblazoned house. Nevine noticed that Dr. Viliček had Novak's notebook tucked under one of his arms.

Xanthae sighed, the resignation and exhaustion in her voice clear. "I knew that you wouldn't have been far from this travesty, Viliček. I don't suppose I could convince you to throw that book into the fire where it belongs?"

"This book," —Dr. Viliček patted it lovingly with his free hand— "contains notes on some of Mr. Novak's most remarkable experiments. Quite dangerous in the wrong hands, as I think you'll agree." He tapped Novak with his foot, and the exhausted and bleeding Novak fell to his hands, collapsing onto the snowy pavement.

"What will you do with him?" Xanthae asked, warily.

"Oh, you can rest assured that poor Novak will get the justice he deserves," Viliček said with an almost kindly grin.

"We'll not let you kill him!" Petyr shouted defiantly. He raised his flamethrower, and the tall blond man raised his pistol, as well. For a moment, they all were quiet, staring at each other as if each group were daring the other to move.

"Come now," Dr. Viliček said at last, smiling calmly as if nothing could make him worry, "there is no need for us to be at odds with each other. Dr. Halruaa, your shoulder needs tending, and I suspect that your young ward," —he gave Nevine a grandfatherly wink— "has seen quite enough excitement for one night."

Xanthae looked at Viliček, but she held up her good hand for Petyr. "You can turn off the flamethrower, Petyr," she said with some reluctance. Petyr looked uncertain for a moment, but dutifully turned the valve on the methane burners until they went silent. The blond man relaxed as well and, tucking his pistol into the waist of his pants, began to hoist the limp Novak up and into the carriage. Xanthae's voice was almost a growl as she said, "I'm sure you understand that you and I are far from done, Dr. Viliček."

"I'll look forward to you dropping by anytime, Dr. Halruaa," he replied pleasantly, as if he hadn't understood the meaning of her comment. "Good night to the three of you."

Viliček climbed into the carriage after the tall blond man and the unconscious Novak. A moment later, they rode away, leaving Nevine, Xanthae, and Petyr alone. By now, there were people in the street with buckets of water tending to the fire. There wasn't much to be done for Novak's home but to manage it so the fire didn't spread to the nearby dwellings. The three of them had neither the energy nor the resources to be of much help in that effort.

Silently, and exhausted, they began the long, cold walk back to Vysehrad. Looking like they did, it seemed improbable that any carriage would stop for them. Worse, they all felt as if victory had been stolen from them. Although the Ghoul of Vysehrad had been destroyed, Novak's notes had fallen into Dr. Viliček's hands and there could be no telling to what purpose Dr. Viliček would put Novak's research.

Looking up, Nevine noticed Petyr had lost his top hat and instead saw the most curious thing. His right temple had a bald spot, a most surprising thing to see. Perhaps the hair had been singed away in the burning house, although she didn't think so. It looked familiar too somehow, although as she was so tired for the moment, she couldn't think of where she had seen it.

"I am sorry it did not turn out as we had hoped," Xanthae said at last, her voice soft.

"We destroyed the ghoul," Petyr said, always the most optimistic of them. "And we all got out alive. I don't think that's too bad."

"Petyr's right," Nevine said.

"We destroyed the ghoul because he stood there and let us destroy him." Xanthae sighed. "I owe you another thank you, Nevine. You've saved my life for the third time and how long we have known each other?"

"A week, I think." Nevine blinked, looking up at Xanthae. "You've saved my life twice…once that first night and again in the crypt."

"Ahh…" Xanthae said, nodding, "so I owe you just one more."

"Maybe if you take me to get some of those Czech pastries, we'll call it even?" Nevine smiled.

"Oh, you like Trdelnik, do you? I think we may have a few days to relax and see if we can find a shop in the city."

215

After a few moments of walking, they heard a carriage approaching from behind them. They stopped and watched as it drew up next to them, and the passenger slid open a little curtain to address them. It was the mayoress, a woolen coat wrapped around herself to stay warm. Her golden hair and eyes sparkled in the light from the fire at Novak's home.

"Good evening," said the mayoress coolly. "I see that you have completed your mission with your usual subtlety, Dr. Halruaa." As she said this, there was a crash from down the street as the roof of Novak's home fell in. The mayoress did not turn her head to look at it.

Xanthae had difficulty keeping her dislike of the mayoress from her expression or tone. "Bad news certainly travels quickly in this city."

"Bad news?" the mayoress sounded mildly surprised. "I have it on good authority that you have destroyed the Ghoul of Vysehrad and taken its creator out of commission. Who would ever have suspected that Novak would have been behind it the whole time?" It was difficult to tell if the mayoress' tone was sincere.

"Then I assume you have heard as well that Dr. Viliček has taken Novak's notes. You know as well as I that he'll use them in his own research." Xanthae sounded earnest, but also as though trying to reason with the mayoress.

The woman waved a dismissive hand, though. "You worry too much about that doddering old man. He's harmless, if a bit eccentric. I have something for you that will brighten your mood." The mayoress dangled a small purse out the window with her thin, pale fingers and jingled it a few times so that it was obvious to all that it was filled with coins. After a moment, she threw it at Xanthae's feet. Xanthae hardly looked at it, her expression one of distaste.

"It's your bounty, as promised!" the Mayoress exclaimed. "For your fine service to the people and city of Prague." When Xanthae still made no move to retrieve the coins, she added, her tone a little threatening now, "Dr. Halruaa, I think we can all speak plainly here and acknowledge that on your Imperial Stipend, it must be hard enough to feed one extra mouth." She made a dismissive motion toward Petyr. "Now having to worry also about a second, albeit very clever, young mouth to feed." The mayoress smiled at Nevine and that smile gave her a deeper chill than the night's air ever could.

Looking as if she had been asked to pick up a dead kitten, Xanthae bent down and retrieved the little purse. "So long as we understand, I don't owe you anything more for this."

"Dr. Halruaa, you'd always be so much more interesting outside my sphere of influence than within it." The mayoress flashed the three of them a satisfied smile. "I'd offer you a ride back home but, frankly, you're filthy. Good evening to you all." With that, she drew closed her curtain and the carriage drove on past them, moving gradually out of sight. The three of them watched it go before silently resuming their long, cold walk back to Vysehrad.

****

That night, Nevine slept in Xanthae's bed with the woman's good arm snuggling her. Nevine had used the pretext of keeping a good watch on Xanthae as she healed, but they both knew that wound to Xanthae's shoulder had required only a few stitches, and too much had happened for Nevine to sleep alone comfortably.

"I'm very proud of you," Xanthae whispered to her while they were still awake late at night.

"I'm very proud of you too," Nevine whispered back, smiling. "Thierry Grimoire's ghost was in Grimoire Manor when I was there last time. He called me Sophie even though I wasn't wearing the necklace. I wonder why he did that."

"Perhaps after the first time he saw you with the necklace here, you just became Sophie to him. Or perhaps he knew you were not Sophie all along. But caring for you like he would his sister was the one good thing he was capable of during his most evil reawakening."

"It's not over for him yet," Nevine said sadly. "His soul is still miserable. So is his mother's soul, Genevieve. Neither of them will be at peace until he forgives her, I think."

Xanthae was quiet for a moment before she said, "You will take care of them in Newport, won't you?"

"I'm going to try," Nevine said uncertainly. "Dr. Halruaa…I wonder if I came here, or was sent here by God or something, or however I got here, to help Thierry and Genevieve Grimoire, I'm afraid that when I do help them, I won't come back here again." There were tears in her eyes as she said this, indeed, as she spoke out loud her worst fear.

Xanthae's own eyes seemed to be watering up a bit in the flickering candlelight as she stroked Nevine's hair. "You might be right about what brought you here. I think though that you and I have many adventures ahead of us yet. That is one thing I feel most certain about, Nevine Turner."

"Do you promise?"

"I promise," Xanthae whispered, and with those words, Nevine felt an utter calmness that at last allowed her to close her eyes and to fall asleep.

Chapter 17

Sophie

This time, Nevine was not at all surprised to wake up back in Newport. This flip seemed inevitable, like the necessary end of a spectacular journey. There was a tug of sadness as she woke, realizing that, despite Xanthae's assurances, she could never be sure if and when her flips to Prague might end. She realized perhaps this was why some souls became lost on Earth after death: life was so precious to them that they hung on somehow after death, fearing what might come next. All journeys, even the best ones, came to an end, though.

Nevine went through the motions while attending classes, although her mind was on other matters. She discovered she had gotten a C- on her history test, which was not terribly bad given how distracted she had been since her arrival at Grimoire Manor. Aurora managed to pull a C+, and Nevine was sorry to think she was causing her friend to get less-than-stellar grades. From the big smug smile Fiona Applegate wore, she could only guess her nemesis had gotten an A, probably with some kind of a stupid sticker on the front of the test. Ms. Donitz spent ten minutes berating the class for their lackluster performance, although it was obvious to the whole room that Fiona was immune from the criticism.

After class, Nevine visited Ms. Emily again. There was no particular reason other than a chance to see Joshua, if only for a few minutes.

"Well this is a nice surprise, Nevine," Ms. Emily said with a bright smile. During class, Ms. Emily still called her 'Miss Turner' like all the other teachers, but after class, she switched to 'Nevine'. She liked being called by her first name better. Being referred to so formally all the time made her feel like she was always in trouble.

"I was wondering if I could look in on Joshua for a few minutes?" Nevine asked, deciding to go for the direct approach.

"Sure. We actually have to leave for a doctor's appointment in a few minutes, but if you want to say hello, that would be fine. He's in his bedroom, as usual."

Indeed, except for the change of clothing, Joshua appeared to be just as Nevine had left him, sorting shiny rocks from one pile to another. Ms. Emily announced Nevine's arrival to Joshua, who naturally ignored the announcement. Ms. Emily then left them to go and attend to some chores.

Nevine knelt beside Joshua, feeling an odd burst of energy and excitement as she did so. As he had done before, Joshua treated her as if she were invisible.

"Joshua?" she said quietly, watching him as he ignored her. If he heard her voice, he gave no indication of it.

"Joshua?" she said again, a bit louder, in case he hadn't heard her.

There was still no sign that Joshua knew she was

there. He continued sorting his rocks back and forth into little piles.

"I see you're sorting your rocks into piles," Nevine said, making small talk, wondering if she could draw him into conversation. She peered at the rocks, wondering what was so special about them that got his attention so much. Why did he care so much about them that he would ignore the rest of the world?

"Do you have a favorite rock?" she asked, wondering if talking about his favorite topic would help. It didn't, and he still ignored her. "I like that shiny one that has the little gold specks in it," she said, pointing it out. He didn't touch the rock or turn to look at it.

Nevine, excited, felt as though on the edge of a very important discovery as she tried what she had intended to try. Whispering now, feeling a bit shy about it, she said, "Petyr?"

He stopped sorting his rocks at once, and looked over at her, his eyes meeting hers very plainly. It was as if he was seeing her for the very first time and appeared to be utterly fascinated with her.

Nevine's heart beat fast with the thrill of discovery. She wasn't sure what this meant, but had suspected something like this might happen. When she had seen Petyr without his top hat, she had noticed his bald spot but hadn't made the connection. Now it seemed so painfully obvious, although she couldn't imagine how Joshua and Petyr were linked together.

"Can you hear me, Petyr?" she asked him.

"Can you hear me, Petyr?" he repeated for her, even matching the Czech accent on the name.

"Petyr, is it you?" she tried again, confused by his

repetition.

"Petyr, is it you?" he repeated once again with a look as if conversation was a most fascinating stranger to him.

Nevine was a bit disappointed now, although she still thought this had been an important discovery. She had hoped, well…perhaps she might have been able to communicate back through to Prague somehow, through Joshua, but that had obviously been a bit of an extravagant fantasy. However, he had responded to the name of Petyr.

"It's echolalia," Ms. Emily said from the doorway, startling Nevine. "He doesn't speak much, but when he does speak, he tends to repeat what he hears. Still, that was very good, as he rarely responds to most people at all. He must like you. What made you call him Peter?" Ms. Emily pronounced the name without the Czech accent.

Nevine shrugged, knowing the real answer would be unbelievable. "He reminds me of someone I know with that name."

Ms. Emily seemed genuinely pleased to see Joshua speaking with her, even if it were just repeating her words. "I'm afraid that we'll have to get going for his appointment, but I do hope you'll come and speak with him again. I can make some pastries or cookies to help entice you."

This made Nevine think of Trdelnik, in which there was little chance of Ms. Emily cooking up, of course, and Nevine became homesick for Prague. She bid them goodbye politely and joined Aurora outside.

"You're going to go back up to the graveyard, aren't you?" Aurora asked after she had been brought up to speed.

Nevine nodded. "I think I have to. Thierry and Genevieve were both in the graveyard when I was there last time, I'm sure of it. If I can get them together again, maybe Thierry will be able to forgive her. It's the only thing I can think of."

"I'm going back up there with you," Aurora said in a determined tone.

"You don't need to. You almost got killed up there once already—"

Aurora held up her hand to cut her off. "That's exactly why you need someone watching your back. You do your little therapy session with your two little ghost friends, and I'll watch your back to make sure the Attic Specter doesn't sneak up on you."

"Thanks, Aurora. You're a great friend."

Staying up late in order to track ghosts and break about a thousand Grimoire Manor rules was becoming such a regular occurrence that Aurora and Nevine weren't going to know what to do with themselves if things ever settled down. Somewhere just before 2 a.m., they were back at the cemetery, hot on the heels of the Hallway Ghost. The cemetery itself looked much as they had left it, including the damaged door to the crypt of Genevieve and Lyrre Grimoire.

"I wish there was something we could do to fix that," Nevine observed. "It looks like someone vandalized it."

"Someone *did* vandalize it," Aurora reminded her, "and tried to get me killed."

They stood on the edge of the cemetery for a minute, clearly lacking a plan. "So now what are you supposed to do?" Aurora asked. "I'm not hopping back into that crypt to get the Hallway Ghost all riled up again."

"Okay, just stay here. I'm going to try something." Nevine walked forward into the cemetery and approached the crypt of Genevieve and Lyrre Grimoire. The iron door hung awkwardly from a single hinge. Beyond, she could see the still disturbed sarcophagus of Genevieve Grimoire. "Genevieve!" she called. "I want to talk to you! I've seen your son, Thierry, in Prague!"

There was a pause for a moment, and Nevine thought perhaps that nothing would happen save for herself looking foolish talking to a crypt. Then the hairs on her body felt like they were trying to stand on end, and an almost electrical hum circulated in the air. Nevine looked around and saw nothing out of the ordinary. All of a sudden, there was a roar from Genevieve's crypt as if a bomb had gone off. Nevine was knocked onto her back by a rush of cold air powerful enough to tear the iron door off its last hinge and send it flying like a deadly discus over Nevine's head. Had she still been standing, the door would certainly have killed her. It landed with a heavy thud a dozen feet behind her.

Aurora rushed to her side while she lay stunned on the cold ground. "Are you all right?"

"I think so," Nevine said, sitting up and looking around. As had happened on the night before, strong winds were beginning to whip up around them, swirling leaves and dust into stinging clouds. "That wasn't quite the reception I had hoped for."

"No?" quipped Aurora. "I thought that went swimmingly."

"I wonder if that was Genevieve or the Attic

Specter?" With Aurora's help, Nevine got to her feet.

"Doesn't really matter much, does it?" Aurora said. "We know that the Hallway Ghost doesn't like loud noises when she's sleeping. She's crankier than I am."

The sound of footsteps from behind caused them made to turn. Emerging from the cliff trail were Fiona Applegate and Jo-Beth. The two newcomers stopped when they saw Nevine and Aurora, and surveyed the damaged crypt. Fiona exclaimed, "Oh my word, Cop-Girl, look what you've done! You'll be expelled for sure for this, probably thrown in jail!"

"I'm a Copt, not a cop!" Nevine yelled back, then shook her head. This was hardly the time for that argument.

"What are you two doing out here?" demanded Aurora.

"I could ask you the same!" Fiona retorted. Jo-Beth stood by, arms crossed, letting her boss do all the talking. "We heard you two sneaking out and figured we'd see what kind of trouble you were up to so we could tell Ms. Speer."

"Well, you're sneaking out too, aren't you?" Aurora pointed out. "So you can't tell her anything without turning yourselves in too!"

"We didn't destroy that crypt!" Fiona screamed.

"We didn't destroy it either!" Aurora screamed back.

"Hey, guys..." Nevine tried to interject but not loud enough.

"Well then, who did?" Fiona demanded.

As if on cue, the heavy stone top of Genevieve Grimoire's sarcophagus was pushed off onto the floor of the crypt and landed with a loud crash. All four girls stopped their bickering and turned to look at the crypt with wide eyes.

"Technically," Nevine said with a false calm, "I think it was the Attic Specter that did the damage, not her, but I think this is as good a way for us to refocus as any."

As they watched, a cloud of dust seemed to sweep out from the inside of Genevieve Grimoire's sarcophagus and moved out of the crypt into the open cemetery. Nevine realized this wasn't dust at all, but a kind of luminescence, as molecules in the air itself were excited and gave off soft light energy. The swirling form that glided out of the crypt looked like a sort of aurora borealis. Only, as they stared at it, it seemed to try to coalesce into human form, with arms and legs and a face. It was less than successful, although it did manage rough pseudopods for limbs, and eventually a distinctly female face of a young woman. Although, it was not detailed enough to decide if it was a young Genevieve Grimoire. The expression on the face, though, looked pained and tortured. The face stared at the four girls, and then opened its mouth in what was obviously a long, anguished silent scream. The air immediately came alive with an electrical charge that set their nerves all on edge.

Genevieve Grimoire was not done yet in unleashing her anger. There were more sounds from within the crypt, and Nevine and Aurora had a good idea as to their source. Their fears were confirmed when a moment later, the corpse of Genevieve Grimoire pulled itself out of its sarcophagus and began to slowly stalk in the direction of the four girls. All that remained of Genevieve was her skeleton, some dried skin, and tattered remnants of what once was an elegant dress. The skull grinned at them in its toothy grimace and stared through vacant sockets. Her bony arms extended out, already reaching for the girls, and it was obvious that if Genevieve's apparition was helpless to do more than scream, she was intent on using her old body to tear them apart.

Fiona and Jo-Beth were both staring with open mouths at the undead Genevieve Grimoire. Aurora was quicker to take action. "I've had enough of you, you old bat!" she yelled at Genevieve and managed to retrieve a good-sized stick from the ground. She put herself between Nevine and the skeleton, intent on heading Genevieve off, and turned her head quickly back to say, "Do whatever it is that you have to do. I'll hold her off."

The trouble, of course, was that Nevine wasn't really sure what she was supposed to do. The other night, though, here in the cemetery, Thierry Grimoire had been here, she was sure of it. His spirit had been timid, lingering on the edge of the woods, and she had to try to draw him out in hopes that he could reach out to his mother. "Thierry!" Nevine called, hoping her voice might be able to do something.

By now, Genevieve's spirit appeared to have learned how to control the skeleton better, and as the corpse reached Aurora, the two of them engaged in a desperate melee. Aurora swung out with her stick and it connected with the skeleton's side with a sound like striking a piñata. The skeleton seemed barely to notice the blow, however, and got its talons on Aurora's shirt. Aurora was picked up off the ground and flung several feet away, landing hard on one ankle with a cry of pain.

She scrambled to get away, but it was plain to see she was having trouble standing and the skeleton would have little trouble tearing her apart now.

At that moment, perhaps the most miraculous thing of the entire evening happened. Fiona turned to Jo-Beth and said simply, "Come on!" and the two of them picked up sticks of their own and descended on the skeleton, keeping it from attacking the wounded Aurora. Nevine had mostly expected Fiona and Jo-Beth to turn and run, and would not have been terribly surprised had they even taken the skeleton's side, but to see them actually helping was nearly too much for Nevine to believe. Ghost and walking skeletons, time-travel and secret societies in Prague were all one thing, but Fiona Applegate being useful was almost too much to process.

With the skeleton distracted, Nevine had a few moments to try to call on Thierry. Not sure even where to face, she called out into the howling wind, "Thierry! Remember what I told you in Prague! This is your chance!" and she continued like this for several minutes.

At last, through the whipping leaves and dust, Nevine saw another apparition forming on the edge of the cemetery. As she watched, it congealed into something of a vaguely male shape, as with Genevieve's ghost, too wispy to be sure it was Thierry. She heard his voice, though, as he said, "Sophie..." and the name was carried to her ears across the wind.

The expression on Genevieve's face changed from anguish to one of confusion and sorrow. She stared at the new apparition, unmoving, clearly uncertain what to do. So many years she must have paced the halls of

Grimoire Manor, wishing that she could have undone her sins; at last faced with them, her soul panicked and froze, much like any living soul would do.

Thierry's apparition moved slowly toward her, drifting over the dormant grass, ignoring the wind and whipping detritus. He approached the ghost of his mother and Nevine could see that his expression was peaceful, sad in a way, but peaceful. As she had hoped most of all...forgiving. If there were any words shared between the ghosts of Thierry and Genevieve Grimoire, Nevine could not hear them, or in their close swirling masses, could she determine any form of communication passing between them. The skeleton of Genevieve Grimoire, though it still stood, had ceased fighting, and the three girls backed away from it, Aurora still trying to crawl along the ground. They all watched as Genevieve extended one of her long, ghostly arms toward Thierry Grimoire. Without hesitation, he reached out one of his own ghostly arms to take it.

The electrical charge in the air intensified immediately—at first warm in the radiant glow of love and acceptance from the reunited spirits of mother and son. This was immediately replaced with a cold wave of sheer rage and hatred as a third entity made its presence known. The ruined crypt door, cast aside on the ground, now began to rise on one side and slam down repeatedly against the ground like a child having a tantrum. A powerful fist of cold air knocked Nevine in the center of her chest and sent her sprawling once again. She could hear a faint but long, echoing scream of utter and pure evil. As the scream faded, the corpse of Genevieve Grimoire spun apart as if a grenade had been set off inside her chest, and the four girls did their best to duck away from the stinging bone fragments that filled the air. Not one of the four was left to doubt that the Attic Specter was not at all pleased to see its plans for the evening, which had likely involved teenage girls killed by an enraged Genevieve Grimoire, go horribly wrong.

As Nevine pushed herself up off the ground, she could see that the spirits of the Grimoire family were finally spent of energy. The apparitions of Genevieve and Thierry Grimoire were now gone, and Nevine had good reason to suspect they would not return. The electrical charge that had emanated through the air died away, and though the Attic Specter was now silent, Nevine knew that whoever he or she was, they had not gone peacefully like Thierry and Genevieve. Even the terrible breeze died away and they were left with a still and cold October night.

Fiona wore a disgusted look on her face as she plucked bone fragments from her long blonde hair. "I can't believe what you've gotten me into, Cop-Girl!"

Nevine rushed over to Aurora to check on her wounded friend. Aurora was able to stand with Nevine's help, but she had sprained her ankle, unable to put much weight on it.

"Are you sure it's not broken?" Nevine asked.

"I can wiggle the toes and move the foot," Aurora answered, grimacing. "I think that means it's not broken, right?"

"Right," Fiona said, walking over to them, somehow fully composed and reeking of confidence. "If you can move it, it's just a sprain."

"Thank you, Fiona," Nevine said. "You really

helped us out tonight. You too, Jo-Beth."

"Yes, thank you, Fiona," Aurora mumbled, as if the words were sheer poison.

Fiona puffed herself up, intent on not taking their words with grace. "Yes, well, I suppose you two owe me one, and you can be sure that I won't soon forget it. And don't think this changes anything between us, Cop-Girl," Fiona warned, and she summoned enough venom behind it that whatever flickering ember of warmth Nevine felt for Fiona was immediately extinguished.

Fiona brushed bone dust off her dress and gave Aurora a critical appraisal. "Cop-Girl, you better get your friend back to Grimoire Manor and get her to Nurse Jodl." She looked over at Jo-Beth, who had been watching the exchange stoically. "Jo-Beth and I will try to clean things up out here as best we can, so you don't get us all expelled."

Nevine managed another, much less enthusiastic "Thank you," but Aurora simply stuck her tongue out once Fiona had turned away. Slowly and cautiously, Nevine lead Aurora down the cliff trail away from the cemetery. Aurora flinched with each step but tried to wear a brave face.

"Except for Fiona being a twit, that was really quite brilliant!" Aurora said between breaths as they laboriously made their way down the hill. "I don't know how I'm going to get to sleep at night without the Hallway Ghost's footsteps lulling me into terrifying nightmares."

"You were the brave one, fighting that skeleton by yourself to protect me. I owe you a big one."

"That was the only thing I could do," Aurora said.

"You were the one who had to get Thierry Grimoire there. Do you think Grimoire Manor will seem less haunted now?"

"I don't know." Nevine realized she doubted that would be the case very much. "I think the Attic Specter is still very angry at us. I can only imagine how many other Grimoires are lurking in the various corners of the house." In a way, her fears were confirmed for, as they neared the mansion once again, she could feel the same uneasy hatred from the building that she had felt the first time she had set foot in it. In that sense, nothing had changed. "We helped Thierry and Genevieve Grimoire, though. I guess that's something."

Nevine set her hand on the doorknob and instead found it pulled out of her grip as the door opened from the inside. Waiting for them with a most displeased expression was the Provost, hands on her hips, still dressed in her business dress as if she never slept. Caught in the moment of their triumph, the two girls sheepishly entered the mansion and shut the door behind them.

"Well, Miss Turner and Miss Ziniti, it's a surprise to find you two awake and cavorting off grounds at this hour. I don't suppose either of you has permission to be wandering off campus?"

Both girls kept quiet, heads bowed.

"Miss Turner, I'm disappointed in you in particular…" The Provost's voice dripped dangerously with venom. "…as I am sure that I forbade you from wandering into prohibited areas on pain of expulsion. What am I to do with you now?"

As much as she disliked Grimoire Manor, the thought of being expelled and forced back into the foster care system was even more frightening. At least at Grimoire Manor, she seemed to have some kind of purpose in hunting the ghosts. Thinking quickly, and feeling a momentary surge of bravery as she had once before with the Provost, she said, "Actually, Provost, ma'am, you warned me never to go into the attic specifically or else I would be expelled. You never mentioned anything about any other locations."

Aurora gave her a look as if she had just stuck her head into the mouth of a tiger. It was, after all, a technicality and nothing more.

The Provost straightened up and regarded Nevine with a devilish gleam. At last, she said, "You like to play by the letter of the law, do you? Just be careful that you read the laws carefully or one day they will come back to haunt you." She regarded the two girls with distaste. "Very well, then, against my better judgment, I suspect that two weeks of detention and loss of all outside privileges ought to suit as a punishment, unless you have any other loopholes that you'd like to point out for me, Miss Turner?"

Even if there had been, Nevine was getting a gradual sense of how far it was possible to push the Provost. She shook her head. "No, ma'am."

"Very well, then get this one to Nurse Jodl. She won't be at all pleased to see you at this hour." With that, the Provost walked away.

Nevine and Aurora stared at each other for a moment, knowing that, despite their detention, their salvation had been nothing less than miraculous.

"I thought you were insane," Aurora exclaimed once the Provost was out of sight. "I thought you'd done us in for sure, but that was just the thing, wasn't it?"

Nevine shrugged. "I get the impression the Provost admirers guts, so long as you don't push it. Come on. Let's get you to the nurse."

As they hobbled away, Aurora thought out loud, "Odd, you know...you'd think she'd at least close that loophole...explicitly forbid us from going back to the cemetery. I have trouble thinking she'd forget and give you the chance to wiggle out of trouble again." It was a good point, but there was no way for them to know why she hadn't threatened them with expulsion if they returned to the cemetery. For the moment they were just glad they had emerged from the evening with only minor injuries and detention.

****

Exhausted, they fell asleep later that night with barely a word to each other. Nevine climbed into bed with her fox, feeling a profound sense of accomplishment and relief that she had passed through several important events without being seriously harmed. Lingering in the background of her thoughts, though, was a nagging sense of doubt, as if she had just scratched the surface of a very terrible secret, managing to do little more than to make powerful forces aware of her existence.

That night, her dreams were terrible ones. In the first one, she was walking in the grass outside of Grimoire Manor when she happened upon a praying mantis. It must have been summer in her dream, for the skies were bright and the air warm. She had been curious about the praying mantis and wished to study it up close. In her haste to catch the praying mantis, she managed instead to kill it, discovering only then that the mantis had been eating a nest of stinging ants. She had watched the ants, deprived of their predator, multiply with great speed and spread throughout the Grimoire Manor mansion, stinging the other girls in their sleep and causing great harm.

It was the last dream of the night that Nevine remembered most vividly and which terrified her greatest. In it, she had sailed along the halls of Grimoire Manor as if she had been one of the spirits. Actually, it had been more as if she had been watching the prowling of one of the spirits itself from behind the vantage point of its own eyes. She had been able to feel the terrible hatred that coursed through the spirit's soul as it had predated the halls. The spirit had felt almost impotent, wishing to lash out, to destroy, to kill, but unable to do so, having no body. The spirit managed to pass through from the main hall into the girls' dormitory, and it had felt a terrible sense of triumph, as if it had never been allowed there before. One of the doors had been left open, not by much, but enough to allow for the passage of an apparition. The room had belonged to a girl whom Nevine didn't know.

Nevine had watched through the spirit's own eyes as it had hovered over the girl's bed as she slept, innocent in her ignorance of the danger that stalked her. Only at the last minute, perhaps awakened by the sudden cold, had the girl awoke and looked up with shock and terror in her eyes. At that moment, the apparition struck, rushing in at the girl before she had the chance to open her mouth to scream. The last thing she could see was the specter's amorphous arms reaching out for the girl like the rays of the Black Sun.

Nevine awoke with a scream of her own, and her

body almost instinctively lurched into motion, as if trying to recoil from the terrible specter in her dreams. "Aurora!" she shouted into the utter darkness. "Aurora!"

She pulled herself, panicking, out of her bed, and reached out into the darkness to steady herself. Her shin collided nastily against something hard and heavy, a desk perhaps. Her mind, trying to make sense of familiar surroundings to get oriented, found itself unable to do so, and her panic deepened.

She screamed again, a horrible, desperate, hopeless sound that cut through the night. She reached out again in the darkness, felt something metal spin away from her touch and tumble away into the dark. She felt trapped, confused, and very frightened, wondering why Aurora had not responded to her.

At once, hands were on her shoulders, trying to restrain her. She fought against them at first, lashing out in terror with her fists before she realized that those hands were not trying to harm her but instead trying to calm her. She stopped struggling then, trying to peer through the dark for whomever it was in the unfamiliar room with her.

"What is it, Holubička?" whispered a soft and concerned voice in her ear.

It took Nevine another moment before she realized who it was and where she was. She wiped away one terrified tear from her cheek and said, "Oh, Dr. Halruaa, I think that we've made a horrible mistake!"

A word about the author...

Aside from being an author, Christopher J. Ferguson is a professor of psychology specializing in forensics, an occupation which helps inform his writing. He has worked with a wide range of offender populations, from murders to sex offenders to child abusers. His works include several published short stories in Orion's Child, Nefarious, Midnight Horror, Blazing! Adventures, Stories That Lift and Fantasy Gazetteer. He is also a contributor to Newsweek and Quillette. He lives in Orlando, FL with his wife and young son. http://www.christopherjferguson.com

Thank you for purchasing
this publication of The Wild Rose Press, Inc.

For questions or more information
contact us at
info@thewildrosepress.com.

The Wild Rose Press, Inc.
www.thewildrosepress.com